Iris's book

ARCHELAUS HOSKEN'S DILEMMA

A Cornish Historical Comedy

By

F J Warren

With love
FJ Warren

Other books by the same author
The Trevu Trilogy
Broken Bonds (ISBN 978-184685-208-4)
Familiar Strangers (ISBN 978-184685-311-1)
Hidden Revelations (ISBN 978-1-84685-689-1)

Front cover design courtesy of Justin Hubbard

This novel is entirely a work of fiction. The names, characters and incidents portrayed in it are the work of the author's imagination. Any resemblance to actual persons, living or dead, events or localities is entirely coincidental. F J Warren asserts the moral right to be identified as the author of this work.

Copyright F J Warren 2007

All rights reserved

No part of this publication may be reproduced, stored in a retrieval system, or transmitted in any form or by any means, electronic, mechanical photocopying, recording or otherwise, without the prior permission of the author

British Library Cataloguing In Publication Data
A Record of this Publication is available
from the British Library

ISBN 978-1-84685-819-2

First Published 2007 by
Exposure Publishing,
an imprint of
Diggory Press Ltd
Three Rivers, Minions, Liskeard, Cornwall, PL14 5LE, UK
and of Diggory Press, Inc.,
Goodyear, Arizona, 85338, USA
WWW.DIGGORYPRESS.COM

ACKNOWLEDGEMENTS

The author wishes to thank her family and friends for their encouragement before, during, and after the completion of this work.
Particular thanks go to Joan, John, Jane, and JT for all their hard work on my behalf.

Special thanks to Iris, Jennifer, PJ, and especially Justin for his enthusiasm and invaluable assistance.

For Iris
(A very special person)

CHAPTER 1

ARCHELAUS HOSKEN, suddenly finding himself bathed in the strong sunlight that beamed down upon him, screwed up his eyes in an effort to view his surroundings. After spending two days in Penzance's extremely cramped lock-up, he had not expected to find himself suddenly released. An accomplished thief and pickpocket, he had been disappointed to be accosted, arrested, and thrown into jail as he made his way through the crowds at the annual Corpus Christi fair. With no one to defend him and no defence to offer, he had presumed that he was more likely to be taken to Bodmin for sentencing. Hanging, hard labour, or transportation had all seemed a distinct possibility and with escape an unlikely opportunity, the unlooked-for freedom that he was now being given seemed miraculous in the extreme.

As the sound of a man's voice broke in upon his thoughts, he turned his head to view the speaker. James Trenear, the officer in charge of his incarceration, was addressing a silhouetted figure sitting at the front of a farm cart. The cart had various items of agricultural equipment nestling in the back of it, along with an extremely finely worked leather saddle. His eye gleamed with contentment; whoever owned such a humble equipage undoubtedly had the wealth to purchase an item of considerable worth. Archelaus, a thief all his life, never failed to notice the riches of others, for their prosperity would often have a direct bearing on his own. Although, admittedly, this by his obtaining a portion of their wealth by trickery and theft, than by any charitable means on their part.

"A fool, Miss Polmennor, would 'ave move sense than 'ee, if I may be so bold! You mark my words, this will come back to haunt 'ee!" proclaimed Trenear, in a deep voice, and passed over his former inmate's belongings, a small bundle wrapped in a tattered shawl, to the driver of the cart. Archelaus, his eyes now accustomed to the light, raised his head, the better to view the waggoner, and got the shock of his life. It was not the weather-beaten face of an old harridan that met his gaze, but that of a fresh complexioned young woman. Dark haired and dark eyed, common enough features for the Penwith locality, but the stern expression on the damsel's face intrigued him and, it had to be admitted, he wondered what the woman's reason was that she required his freedom in order to accomplish it.

"Get up!" she said sharply, addressing him. He did as he was told, and as he hoisted his body onto the seat beside her, he was aware that those dark, penetrating eyes never left him.

Once seated, he turned and doffed his battered and crumpled hat, an old tricorn that had seen better days and former glories, and said with a smile, "A pleasure to meet 'ee, Ma'am. May I be so bold as..." but he got no further in his introduction.

"Be quiet!" she ordered, flipping the whip across the horse's back, before addressing the officer. "Good day to you, Trenear," she announced, brusquely, and headed out of the town, directing the cart uphill, in a westerly direction. The officer, doffing his own hat, shook his head in dismay, before turning on his heel and re-entering the dark and dismal establishment that served the purpose of Penzance's lock-up.

The couple in the cart rode on in silence, although both made surreptitious glances at the other, whilst attempting to give the impression that neither occupant had the least interest in the person sitting beside them. At the crossroads, a solitary rider sat his horse and awaited their arrival with a malicious gleam in his eye. A handsome fellow, well dressed and possibly in his mid forties, the disdainful smile on his face only adding to his stature.

"My dear, sweet cousin," he enthused - rather coldly, noted Archelaus. "When I heard of the adventure you had set forth upon, I thought it my duty to accompany you from the town. 'Tis not everyday that Mistress Polmennor would seem to have taken leave of her senses and I would consider myself lacking in my family duties if I did not attempt to offer her some protection."

Hosken felt the lady at his side stiffen and was not surprised to hear the anger in her voice as she replied: "Cousin Richard, there's no need for you to inconvenience yourself on my behalf. I am quite capable of driving myself home without the assistance of a member of my family. In fact, a member of my family offering assistance gives me more concern than confidence!"

Cousin Richard smiled again, but still the warmth was lacking in his face.

"Ah! Sweet little Patience Polmennor, what a mis-named person you are! See what folly you are set upon committing here when a little patience, Patience…" and here Richard chuckled at his own humour, "…would have seen all to rights!"

"Nonsense!" snapped Patience. "If it is your intention to accompany me to my home then I cannot stop you, but do not fool yourself into thinking that you can influence me in my decision or to make me change my mind in any way because, I can assure you, you cannot!" she informed him in a very strict manner.

He bowed in acknowledgement and turned his horse to fall in beside her. Miss Polmennor whipped her horse to a trot, and so conversation was limited by the noise of the objects placed in the cart being thoroughly shaken about and by the rumbling of the wooden wheels over the rough road. It was obvious that Cousin Richard's attempt to influence Miss Polmennor was doomed on this occasion, but it was also plain to see that the man was determined not to be deterred from his object. Whatever the purpose might be, Archelaus Hosken had not the slightest idea, but the whole situation began to intrigue him. Archelaus, devious, crafty, and quick to see a means to improving his own circumstances, felt a shiver of excitement course through his veins. A divided family, lost in their private battle, could well be blinded to any or all of the havoc that Hosken would be capable of causing in their lives. Living hand to mouth had taught him well to avail himself of all opportunities that presented themselves.

As no conversation was being offered, he cast his mind back to the reason for finding himself travelling even further to the west in what was the most western part of Cornwall. Two days previously, he had been attending the Corpus Christi fair in Penzance, happily availing himself of the largesse that the innocent crowds displayed about their person. A watch here, a purse there – 'twas an easy game for an experienced pickpocket like himself to play. All would have been well if it were not for the sudden exclamation of a rather tall, countrified gentleman; a rustic obviously, but of some worth for his purse was heavy, who noticed at once that his pocket was being divested of its contents. Hosken turned to melt into the crowd but, of a sudden, a hand grabbed hold of his collar and his assailant's other arm, burly and muscular, wrapped itself around his body. Hastily, he dropped the purse and stamped his boot on it so as to hide it from general view. Normally, this would have been a successful action for the ground would have been muddy underfoot and the object, squashed into the mud would have been hidden to some degree. With luck on his side, he could have protested his innocence, for he would not have been discovered with this particular victim's property about his person. It was not to be, for his attacker had the foresight to plant his heavy-booted foot on the top of Hosken's, thus trapping purse and the purse-taker's foot completely. The ground itself conspired against him for it was parched and hard, due in the main part to an exceptionally dry spring. The purse lay atop the grass so that it was not at all hidden from view, as the thief had wished. Within a short space of time, Archelaus Hosken found himself removed to the town prison and had his own pockets picked of the misappropriated goods he had obtained that day. Several people came to claim the various items that were placed upon Trenear's sturdy table. They all complained vociferously at the assault made upon them but his captor, the large yeoman, said no word at all, merely regarding Hosken shrewdly.

"You 'ave your purse, Mr Angove?" enquired the jailor.

Angove inclined his head but remained silent. Hosken, not one to miss an opportunity, raised his eyes to the man's face and attempted a friendly smile. 'Best not to annoy the fellow,' he thought to himself. Angove merely raised an eyebrow but turned to Trenear and addressed him calmly, "I 'ave, Mr. Trenear," he said, then reached into it and produced some coins, which he placed on the table.

"See 'im fed, Mr. Trenear," he ordered, "and not that misnamed bowl of mucky water that yer missus do pass off fer soup!" Without further ado, he turned on his heel and left the premises.

After two rather uncomfortable nights in the jail, Archelaus was most surprised to discover that all charges against him had been dropped and that a personage had obtained his release. He did not believe that the rustic would have the authority to gain his freedom for him and could not imagine that any other about the town would have the least interest in doing so. To find himself presented with, he had to acknowledge, a personable young lady, had been quite a surprise. Perhaps a brief sojourn on some westerly farm would reap benefits, he considered. He could easily find his way back to the town and with his ability to steal; he would soon have the necessary wherewithal to rejoin any band of travellers that he happened to come across. There were plenty of markets, fairs, and suchlike, and where crowds gathered, the travelling communities that he had grown up with abounded. They lived off their wits and the crowds, and young Archelaus Hosken, although not born into their families, had learned their trade more by default than breeding. He took a deep breath; he was free and he imagined it would not be long before the open road called him to her again. His companion, whatever her reasons might be, would have little chance of holding him for he had not reached the age of five and twenty without discarding many and more beautiful females from about his person. He did admit to some concern, however, when it occurred to him that the woman sitting beside him had not shown the slightest interest in him. 'What of it!' he reasoned blithely, 'she wished for my release and here I am! If she wishes for pleasure I'll provide it, as for work…' he smiled to himself, 'I might oblige, but as soon as my chance comes I'll be away!' Convinced by his own arguments, he turned and smiled upon his companion.

"Wipe that silly grin off your face, Hosken!" she announced in a crisp voice. Archelaus, convinced of his own ability to charm the female sex, suffered a momentary setback at her tone and his smile disappeared at once. A hard gleam came into his eye but Patience Polmennor seemed not to be at all put out by his expression. She sniffed; "You're rabble, Hosken, but you suit my purpose! But I warn you now, if you don't play the game by my rules you'll find yourself shackled and on your way to Australia or worse, hanging by your neck in Bodmin!" By this time, their equipage had reached the entrance to a lane on the right of the road they were travelling on and, oblivious to the rider at the side of the cart, Miss Polmennor turned the beast into the lane.

"I'll wish you farewell, Patience, my dear," announced Cousin Richard, "but I'm sure I will be delighted by your presence within a very short while."

"Not if I can help it!" Patience threw back at him and without any other form of dismissal, made her way down the lane. Archelaus turned in his seat and regarded their erstwhile outrider. He sat his horse, on the road by the entrance, watching their progress down the lane. His face appeared expressionless but his demeanour gave Hosken the impression of a man filled with anger.

"Am I to meet any other members of your family, Miss Polmennor?" he enquired, in a pleasant voice. "I only ask because it would appear that they be a most…" Again, he found his conversation abruptly terminated by his companion.

"When I ask it of you, speak," she ordered, "for the rest of the time keep your mouth shut! 'Tis not the sound of your voice that made me obtain you."

There was something about her speech that gave Hosken a qualm of concern. It was almost as if he had been freed from one imprisonment to be cast into another. Suddenly, they turned a corner and the lane opened out into a fine farmyard. Passing through it, they came across a house set back against the hedge of a field. A pleasant enough building, he noted, but not out of the ordinary for that area. The door opened upon their arrival and Archelaus caught sight of the tall yeoman who had entrapped him at the fair. 'So the fellow is part of this business, after all' he mused. Just at that moment, a large dog rushed from the house towards the cart. His bellowing bark and manner was alarming, but the thief convinced himself that he could soon befriend the animal.

"Best you stay still!" commanded Miss Polmennor, "for my dog is a most protective beast!"

"I've never come across a dog yet that would not be my dearest friend without the merest acquaintance," Archelaus announced confidently, and without further ado got down from the cart. Immediately, the dog jumped at him, pinning him back against the wagon, his slavering jowls not an inch from

Hosken's face. Although sensible enough not to panic, the thief stood still as stone, more from fear than wisdom.

Calmly, Miss Polmennor got down from the cart, nodding to the yeoman as she did so. She walked around the cart and stood beside the dog, which was still giving the impression of a creature wishful of sinking his fangs into the trapped man's throat.

"Do you ever listen to advice, Hosken?" she sighed in annoyance.

Trying to show a confidence he was far from feeling, Archelaus attempted a reply, hoping desperately that his voice did not quiver with fear as he did so.

"Occasionally, Miss Polmennor," he replied, his voice a trifle high, and licked his dry lips nervously.

"This is Rip," she said, indicating the dog, "so called because when he was young he would rip every item that he came across into small pieces. However, as he has grown this habit has been refined. Now, he shows a tendency to wish to rip the throat from any fool not capable of doing as I would wish! A most comforting protector, is he not?" For the first time since he had met her, Miss Polmennor smiled - at the dog, not himself, but it certainly added charm to her features. Archelaus Hosken nodded in agreement; the dog growled at the action and pushed his jaws closer into the thief's face. Hosken's gulped involuntarily.

"Does Rip respond to commands, perchance, Miss?" he gasped desperately.

"Why, of course he does, you silly man. Surely, you do not imagine that I would bother to obtain your release, bring you all the way to my home, only for my dog to . . . kill you, do you?" and she raised her twinkling eyes to his face, a provocative smile on her lips. Physically, she looked more entrancing by the minute, but with the dog's hot breath fanning his face his immediate concern involved his release from the animal's embrace, rather than contemplating his companion's charms.

"I would be most beholden to 'ee if you could obtain my release, Miss Polmennor," he requested, beads of sweat now running down his face.

"Again, Mr Hosken? To be released twice in one day seems quite an achievement!" and she laughed gleefully. No doubt, his predicament amused her, he fumed in annoyance.

"Please to inform your dog that whatever it is you wish of me, then I will be happy to oblige!" announced Archelaus, hoping that this admission would procure his freedom, and not considering his words in the least.

Miss Polmennor smiled broadly, "Just as I thought, Hosken. You are a most obliging fellow. Cousin Richard need have no fears on my behalf after all!" Turning to her dog, she merely said, "Down, Rip!" in a firm voice and turned away. Immediately, the dog released him, but he had to reach out to grab hold of the cart's wheel to steady himself, for his legs did not seem capable of holding his body upright.

His pride dented but his spirit unbroken, he found his voice and demanded to know what her reason had been to bring him to this out of the way place.

"I have need of you, Hosken," she said simply.

"Then tell me what your need is and I'll be on my way," he said, becoming exacerbated and no longer desirous of availing himself of any of her delights, for Rip had made it clear that any attempt to steal from the property, or even to lay a hand upon Miss Polmennor, would lead to the dog's showing his vicious tendencies again.

She raised an eyebrow at him; "On your way?" she queried, "I think not."

She eyed the ragged man who stood before her, his clothes and now his dignity all in tatters. Even so, the fellow bravely lifted his chin and stared her firmly in the face.

"As I mentioned, I have need of you, Hosken. I have a position that needs to be filled," and she smiled as she spoke. Calmly she continued, seemingly not in least perturbed by what she was saying; "Undesirable wretch that you are, Hosken, I intend to have you as my…" she paused for a brief moment, and Archelaus noticed the look of devilment that she could not keep from her face, "… husband!"

CHAPTER 2

SHOCKED into silence, Archelaus stared as Patience Polmennor turned and walked towards the house, her dog following faithfully at her heels. Angove, standing at his side, reached into the cart and retrieved the tied bundle that contained Hosken's earthly belongings. Catching the bemused youth by the arm, he began leading him in the footsteps of his employer, or at least Hosken presumed that was their relationship. Considering what he had just been told, he felt completely at a loss as to what the situation was in this strange household.

Angove called out, in a firm voice: " 'Enry, take the cart to the barn. When 'tis unloaded take the saddle to the tack room and make sure yer 'ands be clean. Mistress won't 'ave her fine new saddle spoiled with no dirty marks".

"Right you are," responded a voice from behind him, but Angove's companion was busily regarding the back of his prospective wife and found no desire to turn around to see who ' 'Enry' might be.

"Did…did I hear right, Mr Angove?" he asked, desperately trying to get his voice under control.

" 'Ess boy," confirmed Angove, his tone calm and controlled.

"I…I don't think I'm the sort of husband Miss Polmennor be looking for, Mr Angove," he attempted, "for 'tis obvious to me that she's a well-appointed lady and would have no need to look amongst my sort for a spouse."

Angove stopped in his tracks and roughly pulled Hosken around to face him. He glared into the young man's face. "Listen to me, boy!" he demanded, "If Miss Polmennor want 'ee for her husband then thas' what's goin to 'appen! Understand, Hosken?"

"I…I might be married, already," proclaimed Archelaus defiantly.

Angove's face split into a wide smile and he gave voice to a crack of laughter.

"Who the 'ell would marry the likes of 'ee, ya blaggard?" he asked, but before waiting for a reply, turned and resumed their progress towards the house.

"Well, Miss Polmennor seems to want to," responded the pickpocket, if not with pride, at least with bravado.

"Desperate needs require desperate measures!" snorted Angove in disgust. Arriving at the door, he unceremoniously pushed the young man into the hallway, releasing his arm as he did so. A door to his left was open and the pickpocket heard a woman's voice demanding that he attend upon her in the room. Angove pulled the tricorn hat from Hosken's head and pushed it into his hands, with an abrupt: "Mind your manners!" and then, pushing him into the room, shut the door behind the fellow with a resounding slam.

Archelaus, clutching his hat nervously, regarded the lady sitting opposite him in the large, well-appointed chair. Glancing quickly around the room, he noted with a professional interest that the room was not devoid of ornament. Good quality furniture, if a trifle austere and old-fashioned, a carpeted floor and a fine selection of china dotted about on various shelves and tables. However, his survey was curtailed by Miss Polmennor's voice cutting in upon his observations.

"Have you family?" she asked.

"Not that I know of, Miss Polmennor, but I…" Again, he found his speech curtailed.

"You have a most annoying habit, Hosken, of saying more than I require to hear," she snapped. Stung into silence, he regarded her with hostility.

"I can't keep calling you Hosken," she announced. "Tell me your full name."

"Archelaus Hosken, Miss Polmennor," he advised, his voice tight with a simmering anger.

"What a dreadful name," she told him, "that will have to be changed. I cannot possibly spend my life addressing a man as 'Archelaus'!" she informed him in disgust. She thought for a moment. "I know, I shall call you Archie," she stated decisively.

He blinked. He had rarely considered his name, but now that it was to be so unexpectedly taken away from him, he felt most aggrieved.

"I prefer to keep my name, I'll have you know, Miss Polmennor," he announced grandly.

"You may keep it and you may use it, Hosken, but when I address you as a wife must, then it will be as 'Archie'! Is that understood?"

"Yes, Miss Polmennor, but I..." but a raised eyebrow stopped his speech. He glowered at her, noting with an angry flush that she was just as busily engaged in observing him. Miss Patience Polmennor was not a great beauty, but her strength of character gave an exciting, determined look to her features. Of medium height and with a well-proportioned body, it surprised the thief that she would need his services as a husband. She had fine enough qualities to ensure that there would be a large number of men willing to call at her door, especially when he presumed that the farm was in her possession. Many a poor man was prepared to marry for less than this lady obviously possessed.

The lady in question regarded him solemnly. She saw before her a thin, gangly young man. Not particularly handsome but, she noted with approval, he had an engaging smile, with twinkling grey-green eyes. His hair, a rather medium brown shade, was curly and worn long over his collar. His face was unshaven, and a golden down bristled on his firm, well-shaped chin. She considered him rather in the fashion that a farmer might judge a specimen of cattle. A good wash and a visit from the barbers would no doubt improve him considerably, Patience surmised. The face that regarded her with such hostility showed none of the charm that she had noted when she had first caught sight of him, when he had gained his freedom earlier that morning. His youthful charm had shone out of him then, like the sun appearing from behind a cloud. Something within her wished to catch sight of that image again, but she had been brought up from a young age to be mistress of the house and the farm, and such fanciful notions were swiftly swept from her mind.

Recent events had caused her to contemplate matrimony more from necessity than desire. Well aware that prospective husbands in the locality came with baggage, numerous close family and other assorted relations, she shunned their advances with disdain. Orphaned before her tenth birthday, she had acquired a highly developed streak of authority. When her solicitor had arrived that fateful morning, to point out that unless she married before her twenty-fifth birthday, the farm automatically came into the possession of her detested cousin, Richard Polmennor, she had exploded with temper. Furthermore, she would be forced to spend the rest of her life living on the trust that her father had arranged to be set up for her. The solicitor, Mr Bosence, quivered before her and when he returned - emotionally bruised and battered - to his office, he remarked to Mr Rodda, his partner, that any man brave enough to marry that 'hell-cat' as he called her, deserved the best wishes of the county!

Within a week of the news, her cousin had called, and informed her that he had come into possession of a most interesting rumour. Inwardly seething, Patience smiled coldly at Richard Polmennor as he intimated to her that he was well aware of her predicament. In his most brazen manner, he advised her that his own son was unmarried and in dire need of a wife. A solution to both their problems had presented itself before them, he told her, a smirk of triumph on his face. He knew his cousin well enough to know that it would take a brave man indeed to take her to wife. The advantage that his own son had was in the fact that he was something of, as the locals charitably called it, a natural. A difficult birth might have been responsible, Dr Simcott had informed him, or the child might just have been born with a smaller and less efficient brain than others. Either way, Jasper Polmennor had grown up to be a sweet, good-natured youth with the inability to write his own name or to complete the simplest of sums. Polmennor's wife could have obliged him by dying after the birth, for she suffered greatly, but she recovered. She was of a sickly disposition from that time on but showed no inclination to succumb to any life threatening illness. Richard Polmennor, married with a useless son and a permanent invalid for a wife, found himself trapped. He could not divorce his wife, such things were unheard of, and he could not disown his son for he was his only heir. His only chance was to marry the boy off. To do that, he had to find an unmarried lady in considerable difficulty and his young cousin's predicament seemed the answer to his prayers. It would also mean that the estate that his grandfather had so meticulously divided between his own father and Patience's father, would be reunited. To the younger son, Richard's father, had fallen the smaller share; such a circumstance had only added fuel to Richard Polmennor's list of grievances. To get his hands on his cousin's property he was prepared to do anything, but he was well aware that Patience had a will of iron. Expecting to be refused, he had merely smiled when the dismissal came, and left her with the information that he was only thinking of her best interests.

Patience, sitting in her favoured chair, allowed her thoughts to dwell on their meeting earlier that morning. Someone in her household might have informed her cousin of what it was that she had determined to do but in reality, she presumed, it would have been James Trenear who would have passed his knowledge on to his friend, Richard. She sneered derisively. To take a common thief for a husband was unheard of, but such a person could be cowed into obedience; the threat of the hangman would see to that! To marry into a local family meant that Patience would lose most of her authority; to a woman of Miss Polmennor's overbearing personality, such subjugation was more than she could bear to think about.

"Where were you raised?" she enquired of her prospective husband.

"Here, there and everywhere, Miss Polmennor," he replied, "I was taken into a travelling family as a babe and brought up with them. I never knew my real family, although 'twas said my mother was a titled lady and I was her love child." He supplied the last piece of information with a hint of proud defiance in his voice.

"What nonsense!" cried his interrogator dismissively. "Listen to me, Hosken, and listen well. To keep the roof over my head and these lands within my control, I have to take a husband before my twenty-fifth birthday. From a young age, I have been used to having control over my life, and as I do not wish to surrender that control to any man, I have chosen a wastrel such as yourself to marry. Should you wish to refuse my offer, speak now! Trenear will welcome you back, no doubt, and Bodmin jail will be quite prepared to house the likes of you! It will probably be for a short stay; you'll either sail or swing, but either experience will be worse than the life you could lead here, I can assure you! I can imagine that you possess a modicum of good sense, Hosken. You would be a fool to refuse this chance and I think your pride would not let you be thought of as the idiot who turned down Patience Polmennor!"

"Perhaps I would prefer to be thought of as the man who would rather lose his life than his dignity, Miss Polmennor!" he snapped, thoroughly ruffled by her domineering manner.

"Dignity!" she shouted, "What dignity, Hosken? You stand before me in rags, you stink of the gutter and you would be so bold as to talk of dignity!"

He drew himself up, consumed with a burning anger, "You foolish woman!" he retorted, "I can promise to marry you and leave you here with a ring and nothing more than a memory! What makes you presume that I will stay within your reach? Methinks, you are the fool!" In temper, he turned and placed his hand on the door handle. Within a moment, he heard a low growl and felt a tug on his coat. Looking down, he noticed the faithful Rip, his menacing eyes fixed firmly on his face, and his jaws just as securely clamped onto the fabric of his jacket.

Carefully, he released the door handle. He heard a quiet voice call out the dog's name. Immediately, he was freed from the dog's hold and he turned, seething with indignation to face her once more.

"Shall I arrange for the banns to be read on Sunday, Mr Hosken?" she asked, a triumphant smile quivering on her lips.

CHAPTER 3

THE following morning, Archelaus opened his eyes and blinked with disbelief at his surroundings. A pile of straw had been his bed, a large barn his abode and Rip had provided him with company the whole night through. Twice, he had attempted to escape; the first time the dog had growled and held on tight to his clothing, the second time he had grasped Hosken's leg. Rip had not broken the skin but had raised a nasty bruise and Hosken thought it prudent to desist from further attempts to leave. No doubt, an opportunity would provide itself at some time in the future; hopefully before he found himself walking up the aisle with his prospective bride.

"Awake, Hosken?" called a voice from the door. Hosken turned his head. Framed in the doorway stood Angove, his massive arms folded across his chest.

"The mistress will expect you for breakfast when you have made yourself presentable," he informed him, then turned on his heel and walked away from the door.

Yawning, Hosken got to his feet and stumbled out into the yard. By the horse trough stood a chair, and on it lay a towel and a bar of soap. A bowl containing a mirror sat with a razor placed by its side and lying over the back of the chair was a set of clothes. Angove, his arms still folded, stood by the pump at the top end of the trough. A wicked smile crossed the man's face as he intimated to Archelaus that the trough was to be used for bathing. Hosken eyed it with suspicion, never having taken a bath in his life.

"Would it just suffice to wash my face, Mr Angove?" he enquired nervously.

"Get disrobed and get in, Hosken. Miss Polmennor does not like to be kept waiting!" barked Angove. He obliged but complained vociferously all the while. Early morning on a midsummer's day in West Cornwall did not mean that the water would feel any better than freezing. He shivered and tentatively splashed some water over his soiled body. Mr Angove shook his head in disgust, grabbed him firmly by the hair and proceeded to scrub the young felon's skin until it glowed. Hosken, his eyes watering with the cold and the viciousness of Angove's hard-handed treatment opened his mouth to complain. His head was pushed beneath the water and when he was released, he spluttered and coughed as his hair was subjected to a thorough wash. The pump, gushing forth even colder water, was employed to rinse off the lather. Cold and bedraggled, he was instructed to get out of the 'bath' and was given the towel with which to dry himself. Once dry, his new clothes were passed over in the order in which he had to put them on. Half of the garments he had never used in his life and he had to be instructed on how to place them about his person. Angove offered his services to shave him but Hosken resolutely shook his head and, now seated on the chair, performed the act for himself, with Mr Angove helpfully holding the mirror for him. Unfortunately, his ordeal was not yet over; for when he had finished, Angove produced a comb and proceeded to drag it though his tangled hair. With some dexterous use of the razor, he succeeded into forming the young man's previously tangled mop of hair into some sort of order. Correctly assuming that Hosken had no idea how to tie his neckerchief, he did it for him.

"Stand up!" he commanded, and on doing so, Hosken was brusquely informed that his appearance would suffice.

"Follow me!" barked Angove, so Archelaus strode after him, his new boots feeling more comfortable than he assumed they would have. Close on his heels, Rip panted along to complete the group.

In the house, he was taken to a large dining room. The first person that he came across was the housekeeper, Betty Angove, Mr Angove's spouse. As short as her husband was tall, she had an equally domineering manner. They had met on the previous day when he had been presented with a bowl of stew, and an excellent stew it was. He was only given the one bowl, however, and even though he had wiped it clean with the large slice of bread he had been handed, he used all his charm to attempt to convince Mrs. Angove that another helping would be appreciated, though none was forthcoming.

"I'll waste one bowl on 'e, young sir, but you'll earn the rest of your food in this 'ouse!" she informed him with her usual brisk manner.

Cleaning out stables was not an occupation that Hosken had much knowledge of, but Mr Angove ensured that the young man spent the afternoon learning all there was to know about looking after the comforts of the many fine animals kept on the farm. Rip lazed in the sun, seemingly asleep, but there was something about the pricked ears that warned Archelaus not to assume that the animal was unaware of where he was at any one time. By suppertime, Angove's protégé, unused to manual work, was consumed with hunger. This time a fine meal was provided and a quantity of fine ale with which to assuage his thirst, Mr Angove having considered that he had done enough to earn it.

Spending a night in a barn was tantamount to luxury for the young ne'er-do-well; only the companionship of the dog spoiled his night of rest. His desire to be freed from the situation meant that he looked for any available opportunity to abscond and thus free himself from his predicament.

In the dining room, Mrs Angove motioned him to a chair, he bowed and smiled at her but her stern features did not alter. Hosken was beginning to realize that in this household a smile was no guarantee of success. In normal life his breezy, confidant manner and charm had seen him through many scrapes and skirmishes. Here, he would have to find other weapons with which to battle, for he could not win with his charm alone.

He had just sat down when the door opened and Miss Polmennor walked into the room; standing in the doorway, she stared at him without expression on her features.

"Stand up when a lady do come in!" whispered the shocked housekeeper, not expecting to see such bad manners displayed. Archelaus, unaware that he had committed any social misdemeanour, stood up immediately and made a slight bow of his head.

Miss Polmennor's lips twitched for an instance, but Hosken noted the slight movement and thought to take advantage of it. He essayed another of his smiles, but Patience only sighed loudly and said: "Why do you always give the impression of a lunatic escaped from an asylum, Hosken? Forever smiling or gawping at me. Please to desist for I detest it so!" In spite of her unflattering remarks, Miss Polmennor pointed out to Mrs Angove that her future husband had improved considerably from his appearance of the previous day.

"And that awful smell has disappeared, thank goodness!" she sighed with relief.

Taking her place at the opposite end of the dining table, the meal commenced. Hosken, learning by the minute, watched her every action and attempted to copy her. His first impulse, to eat his food with his hands, he curbed in haste as he realized that the silver implements placed on the table were there for a reason. There were too many watchful eyes to fill his pockets with them, so he used them, to the best of his unpractised ability, to eat the food with that he was given. It had to be noted that this time, although she still looked disapproving, Mrs Angove ensured that any amount of food was placed upon his plate. Archelaus, always aware that a meal was not to be despised, ate well. A full belly was a circumstance that he had encountered only too infrequently in his life.

Consequently, the meal was conducted in silence, but he was aware that Miss Polmennor's dark eyes were studying his every action. When she had finished, Patience delicately wiped her lips with her napkin; hastily, although he would have preferred to continue to eat, Archelaus did the same. When his companion stood up to leave the room, he stood up as well and awaited her instructions.

"Follow me," she commanded brusquely.

Dutifully, Hosken followed in her footsteps, noting out of the corner of his eye that Rip awaited him in the hallway. Mistress Polmennor led the way to the room where he had been interrogated on the previous day. This time, Miss Polmennor sat at a small table and indicated that he was to take the seat on the opposite side. He sat down and waited for whatever it was she wished to tell him.

"Can you read, Hosken?" she enquired.

"No, ma'am" he replied

"Have you any knowledge of mathematics?"

He returned the same answer.

"Then I am to presume that you have received no schooling in any form?" she asked, a frustrated edge to her voice.

"That is correct, ma'am."

She sighed in disgust.

"Well, I shall have to ensure that this situation is not allowed to continue," she announced decisively. "I will not have it said that I refused one idiot only to capture another!"

The meaning of this remark was lost on Archelaus, but he was wise enough not to smile. He was fast learning that Miss Polmennor abhorred his attempts at charm. In the circumstances, he thought only of escape, but showing compliance might affect his imprisonment in a more beneficial manner.

"I suppose I could instruct you myself," she remarked. Archelaus, raised his eyebrows hopefully. Some time to ingratiate himself with the lady would no doubt prove profitable to his cause. Surely, with all his abilities, he could soon fool her into a fall sense of security. Making her believe that he was trying his utmost to do as she required, he could seize an appropriate opportunity and take to his heels.

"I would find that most enjoyable, Miss Polmennor," he informed her.

She regarded him with a disbelieving look evident on her face.

"I'm sure you would!" she answered, sharply, "but Angove can instruct you. A modicum of learning will prove sufficient for the likes of you, for it is most unlikely that you will need more ability than to be able to read a document, do some simple addition and sign your name!"

"As you wish, ma'am," he said, and inclined his head to indicate he was agreeing with her request.

"You will have the freedom of the house and farm, Hosken. By all means, use the time available to acquaint yourself with this property," she told him.

His eye gleamed, but dimmed again as she added: "and Rip's companionship, lest you should feel the lack of company!"

She stood up to indicate the conversation was over and with a brisk order to Rip to: "Guard!" she left the room without a backward glance.

Hosken, with a wary eye on the dog, looked about the room again. If he were to avail himself of some of the items, he would have to be careful that he could hide them about his person. With the unlooked for freedom that he had now been given, he took advantage of the opportunity and picked up the silver topped sander that formed a part of the writing materials on the table.

Rip watched him perceptively but made no movement. Hosken smiled. 'Foolish woman,' he thought, 'to leave me here with all these treasures,' and slipped the item into his pocket. The dog growled, stood up and took a menacing step towards him. Hastily, Archelaus replaced the object. During the course of the next ten minutes, he tried, unsuccessfully, to acquire various pieces, but each time the dog gave him the impression that it would be a most unwise course to pursue. Eventually, he gave up, returned to the chair, and slumped into it in disgust.

"Damn creature!" he cursed at Rip.

Suddenly, the door opened and Mr Angove appeared, clutching a slate and a handful of chalk. Hosken eyed him in trepidation. He had no reason to believe that Angove would treat him in any kinder a fashion than he had done when he had been washed earlier that day. However, after two hours of unremitting instruction, it was true that his head ached, but he could write his own name for the first time in his life, recognise and name all the letters of the alphabet and even copy a sentence. Angove was a strict but patient teacher and Hosken had to admit that he found the whole experience enjoyable. Never having been the recipient of any form of schooling he had not expected to be at all interested, but this had proved not to be the case. In fact, he felt a small degree of regret that he would, inevitably, have found a way to ensure his independence before he had been given the time to learn more.

"I will endeavour to assist you with your numbers tomorrow, Hosken," Angove informed him, "but for the rest of the day you may, if you wish, discover the delights of Bosmenna." The look of confusion on Hosken's face brought a smile to Angove's.

" 'Tis the name of the property, Hosken!" he said, and picking up the slate and chalks, removed himself from the room.

Archelaus decided to follow him and noted how quickly the dog fell into step beside him. He directed an obscenity at the creature and Rip, appearing to understand the remark in some instinctive way, returned a low growl by way of reply.

CHAPTER 4

THE following Sunday, Archelaus Hosken found himself the centre of attention when he arrived at the local church as a member of the Bosmenna party. Miss Patience Polmennor walked at his side, her arm linked in his. The Angove's, along with their daughter, Cissy, followed behind. Rip took up his position outside in the churchyard and, seeming in need of rest, promptly fell asleep in the warm sunlight. The poor creature had good need of respite from the continuous attempts of his captive to escape. Archelaus, now given a most splendid room of his very own, had tried to leave it, by way of the window, as soon as nightfall had descended. This time the faithful canine's teeth had drawn blood. The unfortunate young man's anguished cries had awoken the whole household, but Miss Polmennor had done nothing more than to call off her dog and had left him to the housekeeper's tender mercies. It was most unfortunate that Rip's fangs had sunk into his posterior in such a decided manner. Not only had he to display that portion of his anatomy to allow Mrs Angove to clean the wound and apply some salve, an act which was embarrassing enough, but he had to suffer the indignity of having Cissy Angove giggle her way through his ordeal. In fact, when he had yelled in pain as the lotion was applied, poor Cissy howled with laughter and almost dropped the bowl of bloodied water she was holding.

Furious, Archelaus could do no more than accept that for the immediate future, sitting would be an uncomfortable experience. However, he made no more attempts to escape from his room.

The property was a different proposition. Each day he plotted the various escape routes that his practised eye discovered. The dog's growl, and the ever-present pain from his previous attempt, reminded him that he must needs approach the matter with caution. The day before, a golden opportunity had come before him when the cart returned from the field with a large quantity of stones in the back of it. The passage of the cart succeeded in separating himself from the dog, effectively trapping Rip on the far side. Immediately, Hosken turned and ran for the low hedge, scaled it in one desperate leap and, looking over his shoulder to ascertain that the dog was not on his heels, jumped for his freedom into the adjoining field. Unfortunately, he had, in his wisdom, picked the very spot below which lay a large, muddy dewpond. Within ten minutes, he was to find himself sitting in the horse trough whilst he received another thorough clean.

"Hosken, I got admire 'e," a grinning Angove informed him, sluicing off the mud clinging to the bather's hair, "for you be a most determined individual." Various farm hands stood about the yard laughing at his new predicament. Sitting in the freezing water, with the sound of guffaws and laughter ringing in his ears, Archelaus Hosken should have admitted defeat. It was a hard lesson to learn and, although he appreciated that he would have to temper his attempts, to someone of his background it was not a lesson that he particularly wished to accept.

However, he was now at the church and was about to have to listen to his marriage banns being read. Various members of the congregation craned their necks to get a better view of him and there seemed to be an incessant murmur even whilst the vicar addressed the people gathered before him. Miss Patience Polmennor looked resolutely ahead, seemingly without a care in the world. When their names were read out every head turned to stare at them, an uncomfortable experience in itself but the thought of his approaching matrimony Archelaus found even more daunting.

After the service, they stood outside in the sunshine and he was introduced to various members of the locality. His fiancée had already informed him how he had best to conduct himself and, ever aware of the presence of the dog, he followed her instructions to the letter. Knowing the ferocity of Miss Polmennor's demeanour he had no wish to find that Rip would attach himself to some portion of his body should she wish to instruct the dog so to do.

"Naturally, we can hardly wait for the wedding day," Patience thrilled to Mrs. Rodda, "Is that not so, Archie, my dear?" Hosken blinked at her in surprise, but an eye-watering nip in his arm warned him to comply. Hastily, Archelaus nodded his head.

"Quite…um…dearest," he supplied.

Several people came to talk to them and he found himself introduced to almost all the people that were present. Patience Polmennor used the same phrase to each of them, to inform them that it was her dearest wish to be married to Archie Hosken within the shortest time possible. Her manner was pleasant and charming, quite different from the woman that Archelaus knew, but when Richard Polmennor and his party came forwards to meet them, the lady at his side bristled with disgust.

Richard Polmennor, his wife, Sophia and their only son, Jasper, presented themselves. Sophia Polmennor, frail and tragic, regarded Hosken with great nervousness, but young Jasper smiled at him in innocent delight. For the first time since his arrival in the locality, Archelaus Hosken felt a great relief to be in the company of such a pleasant and friendly fellow. Polmennor refused to shake his hand but his son rushed forward and, grabbing hold of Hosken's hand in both of his own expressed his delight at meeting him. A tall, handsome youth, his smile lit up his whole face.

"Hello Archie," he enthused boyishly, "Are you going to marry Cousin Patience?"

Hosken nodded, his own smile brought out by Jasper's genuine happiness.

"Oh good!" he continued with a grin. Then, turning to his father he said: "I won't have to marry Cousin Patience after all because she *has* found a man that will marry her, Father!" His father instructed him to be quiet, but his expression boded ill for his young son's unguarded comment.

"Dearest cousin," he bowed, "such a relief to find you so well. I am sure when the news of your escapade reached my ears I thought to hear of you dead in your bed!" He flashed a look of disgust at Hosken, but Archelaus strove to keep his expressive features under control.

"Why so, cousin?" enquired Patience innocently, "For my betrothed has never shown anything but the greatest desire to please me. Sweet man that he is." Turning to her companion, she bestowed a smile intimating a large degree of love and devotion in respect of his personage.

Bravely, with a wary eye on the watchful canine, Archelaus took her hand to his lips and bestowed a soft kiss upon her fingers.

"Oh Archie!" breathed Patience ecstatically.

"Don't think to fool me with your play acting, Patience. That," and here he pointed a finger of accusation at the young thief, "is a fellow taking advantage of a momentary weakness upon your part. Stop this foolery now! A little sense and a large degree of decorum can solve all your problems and this...this useless wretch can be dispatched to Bodmin to delight the crowds with his dancing jig, no doubt!" he fumed in anger.

"Cousin, I do despair in you," mocked Patience, "Surely you can see how heartfelt my dear Archie's sentiments are for me." Turning to Hosken, she smiled broadly and informed them: "My sweet Archie's feelings for me are often...painful in the extreme. Are they not, dearest?"

Hosken bit his lip and answered in the affirmative. He was somewhat disconcerted by the gleam of devilish glee that danced in her eyes. Archelaus had to admit that when her features were animated in such a way, she looked most attractive.

Richard Polmennor, seething with anger, turned on his heel, throwing his farewells over his shoulder as he did so. Jasper Polmennor, smiling at Cissy Angove with unhidden adoration was instructed to follow him. Immediately a crestfallen expression settled on the young man's face, but Cissy Angove smiled at him and nodded her head. He smiled again, a puppy-like expression of adoration on his features, and turned away. Shaking Archelaus by the hand once more, he wished him and Patience farewell and trotted off after his father. As he passed Rip, he extended his hand. Hosken, expecting the dog to attack the innocent lad, stepped forward in alarm. What he thought to do to save the young fellow, he was not sure, but he felt a surprising fondness for Jasper, and would not have the dog lay his fangs into him. To his surprise, Rip rolled on his back and allowed Jasper to pet and fondle him, the vicious beast that was so familiar to Archelaus transcended into an adoring creature frolicking at the young man's heels. He turned in amazement to Miss Polmennor, but she was smiling at the antics of her dog and the young man.

Again, Richard Polmennor's stern voice commanded his son to follow him and so, regretfully, Jasper patted Rip's head, and ran to catch up with his father.

"I don't believe what I have just seen, Miss Polmennor," breathed Hosken, still astonished at the transformation he had witnessed come over the normally ferocious Rip.

"Rip appreciates innocence, you see, Hosken. A trait that he obviously finds lacking in yourself, yet one he finds in abundance in poor Jasper," she remarked, and continued: "they have been the dearest of friends since Rip was a puppy. Jasper, sweet boy that he is, is not entirely…um," she stumbled over her words. Archelaus broke in at once, saying: "I know what you mean, Miss Polmennor, but he's a fine fellow when all is said and done."

Patience Polmennor studied his face as he watched Cousin Richard's party leave the churchyard. What her thoughts were, she did not express, but there seemed a kinder cast to her features for a brief moment.

After lunch, the young thief went for a walk about the farm, closely followed by his canine jailor. In the garden of Bosmenna, Patience watched as he made his way up and down the hedgerows, smiling at the way he was attempting to discover a route that would enable him to leave the locality the sooner. Thomas Angove's words broke in on her thoughts.

"Hosken's brave, Patience, you've got to admit that, for he would not have Rip hurt Jasper, I noticed," he told her in a fatherly way. In fact, Thomas Angove had stood in the way of father to the girl ever since her own father had died. He knew Patience Polmennor like no other and understood that a marriage of convenience was the most suitable arrangement that she could make. For those closest to her, she showed great love and kindness, but the thought of marrying into a local family appalled her. With good reason, he acknowledged, for they were tight-knit communities and would have used all their powers to control the independent young woman sitting at his side. He had followed the instructions given to him; namely to find a poor man, in dire circumstances, who could be used to stand for a husband to fulfil the terms of her father's will. Admittedly, he had not expected that the solution would be effected with ease, but even he had not assumed that a thief like Hosken would show such determination to quit himself of his impending marriage. Food, a good roof over his head and fine clothing would have appealed to a miscreant of Hosken's upbringing, he thought. So, the pickpocket had been picked out by Angove as a suitable candidate for the position.   Miss Polmennor was in agreement with his choice; the fellow was not trustworthy, it was true, but neither was he seen to display any violent tendencies. Both were surprised that, when offered Miss Polmennor's hand in marriage, the thief showed no desire to accept.

"Brave, yes, but also a fool!" replied Patience with frustration.

She turned to Angove and asked if he thought they would ever be able to get Hosken down the aisle.

"I should think so, Patience. He'll do what you want, for what choice does he have? But he's a traveller through and through and it's breaking him of that habit that will prove the most difficult," he explained. As if to corroborate this statement, they watched in amusement as Hosken made an attempt to abscond yet again. Rip, rolling on his back in the grass, appeared to have forgotten his charge, so the young man clambered up the hedge in haste. The dog, recalled to duty, had him by his booted foot in a trice. Sliding down the hedge in defeat, profuse obscenities were directed at the dog, and the wind took them and carried them to the onlookers in the garden.

"His language is rather colourful at times," remarked Miss Polmennor, a twinkle in her eye.

Angove grinned in reply and watched as the now dejected Hosken made his way reluctantly back to the house.

Thomas coughed in embarrassment before tentatively suggesting that his mistress should show some finer feeling for the fellow. Perhaps this strategy might endear the situation to him, he suggested. Miss Polmennor, an angry blush on her cheeks, remarked sharply that she required a husband in name only.

"If I was looking for love, Thomas, my eye would not be taken by that example of manhood, I can assure you!" she snapped, and getting up from her seat, she removed herself to the house.

Thomas Angove shook his head and sighed. But he understood her reasons well enough. Matrimony was not for the fainthearted after all and Patience had need of a husband she could control. With the ever-present Richard Polmennor sitting and brooding over the iniquities of fate on the next farm, she had to protect her situation most carefully, and if she wished to ensure that she retained control over her life and her finances, a man in Archelaus Hosken's precarious position would appear to be the ideal candidate.

CHAPTER 5

REALIZING he needed to use a new strategy, Hosken had endeavoured to convince those around him that he was, to some extent, complying with their wishes. He resolved not to attempt to escape; indeed the futility of his attempts and Rip's determined efforts in ensuring that he did not, had tempered his desire to have the mad beast sink his fangs into him yet again. So, using his charm, he studiously followed all of Mr Angove's instructions. Consequently, he was allowed a modicum of freedom for his efforts. Rip still continued to follow in his footsteps, but by not displaying any desire to flee, Archelaus wished to fool the creature into a false sense of security. Recognising that he would have great difficulty in absconding from the property, he imagined that his best recourse was to get himself taken to one of the local towns. It would be an easy thing for him to melt into the crowds on a market day, or similar occasion. So, with this object in mind, he applied himself studiously to his education and to any other action that the household wished him to undertake.

There was a heated dispute over the subject of his old clothes, Miss Polmennor wishing for the offending raiments to be burnt for, as she said, he would have no wish to wear such pitiable clothing in his future life. He protested that they were his own belongings and that she had no right to destroy them.

"I think I have every right," she asserted forcefully, "for it is at my discretion that you have your freedom, is it not?"

"Freedom!" he shouted furiously, "You call this freedom?"

"Of course it is, you silly fellow!" she retorted. "What situation do you think you would now be in if I had not acted on your behalf? Sitting in Bodmin awaiting sentence, that's where! In my opinion, this life must be infinitely preferable to the sort of existence you would otherwise be experiencing!" She glared at him, annoyed and disgusted by his attitude and lack of gratitude.

He glared back, angered by her assumption that the comforts he was now the recipient of made up for the independence he was lacking.

Seizing the old shawl, which lay in the middle of the table, she untied the knot and displayed the contents. Another shirt, worn and frayed, a ragged baby's bonnet and a small earring were all it contained. Hosken reached out and pulled the bundle towards him.

"Even in my former life, these were *my* possessions," he fumed, "and treated as such!"

"In this life, Hosken, you have no possessions save for those I wish to bestow upon you, is that understood?" Patience declared forcefully.

At that moment, Thomas Angove calmly interrupted the heated argument.

"If you could see your way to allowing Hosken to keep some of his effects, then perhaps it would be for the best, Miss Polmennor," he advised. "Obviously, some of these items may have sentimental value to Hosken and it would not be fitting to take them away from him."

Patience drummed her fingers on the table in frustration. In her eyes, her faithful Thomas was now siding with her fiancé. She had no wish to find that any future event would compromise her position of authority; Hosken had to know his place, and to be kept in it. She considered, however, that there was some sense in Angove's argument, the young man had been in a more compliant frame of mind of late.

"Very well," she agreed with reluctance. "You may pick out some of the objects that you wish to keep about you, but the rest will have to be destroyed. Surely, you can understand that their condition is not such that they are worth keeping?"

Archelaus scowled at her, but a small light had begun to glow for him. With Thomas Angove's assistance, he had won his first battle with the redoubtable Miss Polmennor. He reached out and put the bonnet and the earring into his tricorn hat. His hand wavered over the old shawl, but he caught her eye and considered it prudent to resist the temptation to claim that as well.

The remainder of the clothes were removed to the yard and Archelaus stood and watched as a flaming torch was applied to them. Dejectedly, he thought to himself that he was saying goodbye to his former life. As his clothing crackled and smoked, he remarked to himself: "She owns me, every damn bit, down to the clothes I stand up in!" Sadly, he shook his head and turned away, but Thomas Angove had heard every word that he had uttered and could not help but feel some sympathy for the fellow. Admittedly, he could not believe that Hosken would not be grateful for his altered circumstances, yet he considered that to find oneself in the position of being under the control of someone of Patience Polmennor's disposition would be a most trying experience.

With the wedding fast approaching, and Hosken's compliant nature being most noticeable, it was decided that a visit to the barbers in Penzance would do much to improve the young man's appearance for when he was to give his vows at the village church.

Two days before the fateful event, Angove took Archelaus to Penzance in the cart. The last time Hosken had travelled in it was when he had been removed from the jailor's custody. He felt anger about all that had happened to him since, but the thought of going back into a town, any town, where he stood a chance of melting into a group of people and getting himself away from his predicament, greatly appealed to him. The dog was with them, naturally, but Archelaus was convinced that the creature could be outwitted easily enough when his nose encountered the many smells that would be about the town.

Mr Bawden, the barber, personally cut Hosken's hair. Renowned as Penzance's finest, for he would not do anything so common as pulling teeth as many of his contemporaries did, he cherished his reputation for dealing with only the higher strata of society. If he considered the former pickpocket to be not the sort of customer he would wish to deal with, he made no remark. The gentleman in question was soon to be the husband of Patience Polmennor and that would prove sufficient to provide an entrée to his establishment. Cut and combed, the young man was led by Angove along the road to Mr Murdoch's shop, only to discover that he was to receive another fine set of clothes. Thomas watched to see if any sign of pleasure crossed the young man's face as his new jacket was placed on his person, the loving hands of the tailor brushing down the cloth with adoration. Hosken looked completely disinterested and Angove sighed in frustration. Ever since he had met the fellow, he seemed incapable of appreciating the luxuries with which he was being showered, his one thought being that he wished to escape his situation. The fact annoyed Angove for two reasons; Patience Polmennor was a fine woman, and her position in society made her a substantial prize for any man to claim. More importantly, he considered that he had found a man who should be overjoyed to have been saved, from a probable early demise, and given so many advantages with which to better his life. He shook his head in disbelief when Hosken, presented with a finely worked pair of leather boots, merely remarked that he already had a pair of boots and could not understand why he should need another, for he could wear only one pair at a time.

Their purchases, carried by the shop staff, were being taken back through the town to the cart when Archelaus espied some people that he recognised. A group of travellers that he had often sought the company of stood by the side of the road. They exchanged glances, but Archelaus and his former companions kept their expressions veiled. The tallest individual in the travelling group nodded his head to indicate to the misplaced thief to follow him, he then began to walk up an alley that lay to the side of Market Jew. Hosken looked about him for a way to escape, desperate to regain his lost life. With Angove at his side and Rip at his heels he was as imprisoned as ever. Then, at last, chance dealt him a favourable hand.

A small child, bowling a hoop with a stick, ran directly in front of Mr Murdoch's assistant and the two collided with considerable force. The shop worker struggled to hold the purchases and the boy, knocked backwards by the shock of the collision, fell over the back of Rip and into the mud of the road, where he commenced to howl loudly. At once, the child's mother appeared and began to berate Mr Angove and his party. Embroiled in the irate discussion, Thomas Angove struggled to keep the peace between the assistant and the boy's parent. Hosken seized his chance and took to his heels, blindly following in the direction that the tall traveller had taken, running up the alley as fast as his legs could carry him. For the first time in almost three weeks, his heart sang. 'I've done it,' he told himself, laughing deliriously as he found himself away from his mentors at last. A small pang of regret caught at his heart as he thought of his meagre possessions, which remained in his room at Bosmenna. They had been with him for most of his life and to leave them was a wrench, but this was his chance of freedom and he had no choice but to take it.

'Old Kelly must be here somewhere,' he reasoned to himself, 'for this is the route that he…' But his thoughts were wiped from his mind as a strong hand reached out and caught him by the arm. He found himself pulled into another alley, darker even than the one he had been running through.

"Agh!" Archelaus cried out in surprise, and then recognizing Kelly, cried out, gleefully: "Michael, 'tis you. Thank God!"

"Pleased t' see me are 'ee, Hosken?" queried Michael Kelly, his tone not altogether friendly.

"Why yes, of course," beamed Archelaus. "If you only knew, my friend, the trials and tribulations I have suffered and how hard I have tried to get away. Where are you staying, for I must be quick? I'm greatly afeared that they will be upon me soon."

Suddenly, the taller man had him by the neck, and demanded his money.

Archelaus laughed, although he felt some fear at the unlooked for attitude of his companion.

"Money? What money? I have only the clothes that you see to my name," he said.

"I don't believe 'ee, Hosken," Kelly growled.

"Mi…Michael, I am destitute!" he protested in growing alarm, "for I have been imprisoned not far from here since Corpus fair. This is my first time in the town since I left the lock-up."

"Left the lock-up?" said the vagabond. "I'd believe a story if you 'ad escaped, but the tale we 'eard was that you was taken into freedom by a young woman. She would appear to be most fond of 'ee, Hosken," and he ran his other hand down the fine apparel that Archelaus was wearing. "Most fond," he repeated in a sinister tone.

"But…but Michael…" stammered the young man, suddenly aware that his appearance gave the impression that he was a gentleman of some means and not the bedraggled traveller that he habitually saw himself as.

Deftly, Kelly ran his hand through Hosken's pockets and quickly discovered to his disgust that not a single coin was to be found on his prisoner's person.

"Why ya wastrel!" shouted the traveller in disgust, "Yer just a bleddy puppet!" and so saying, he drew back his arm and punched Hosken in the face. Archelaus tried to defend himself, but to little effect. He had never been a fighter; his former existence depended on quick wits and his ability not to get caught. Blows rained down upon his face and thudded into his body, Kelly showing little mercy, for he had thought he was to pluck a fine prize when he had enticed Hosken to follow him. His disgust when he discovered that all he had was a useless body in a fine suit of clothes angered him beyond his control. He reached down and pulled out his knife, and catching hold of Hosken's newly cropped hair pulled back his head.

"I'll cut yer strings, ya puppet!" his attacker whispered in his ear.

Hosken lifted his bloodied face and gasped: "Please, Michael, I am not… agh!" but he got not further, as the knife cut into his throat. With the sound of a dog's low growl ringing in his ears, his body slumped to the ground.

CHAPTER 6

WITH great care, Archelaus Hosken's body was removed from the cart and deposited in his room at Bosmenna. Miss Patience Polmennor stood at the end of the bed and viewed with disgust the figure that lay in it.

Thomas Angove coughed in embarrassment, and whispered sincerely: "He's damn lucky to be alive, Patience." If he hoped to engender some sympathy from her, he was to be disappointed.

Miss Polmennor could do no more than stamp her foot in temper, an angry red flush on her cheeks and her eyes blazing fire.

Luckily for Hosken, Rip had been the first to find him and his assailant. Ignoring Archelaus completely, he attacked Kelly with a vengeance, sinking his teeth firmly into the hand that was holding onto his victim's hair. In pain and surprise, the vagabond dropped the knife that he was holding and attempted to fight off the dog. He discovered that he had committed a monumental error in so doing. Rip was ferocious in defence of his charge, as he saw Archelaus, and ripped and tore at the vagabond's flesh with undisguised hatred. Torn and bleeding, Kelly ran for his life. The triumphant canine turned towards the prostrate body, and began to whine and lick at the young man's bloodied features.

When Thomas Angove got to them, Rip was lying by the side of Hosken, pawing desperately at his chest in an attempt to reawaken him. They got him to the doctors with all possible speed and Dr Simcott bathed and stitched the cuts on the young man's face, then sewed the cut on his neck which, thankfully, had not managed to penetrate so far that it had caused a life-threatening trauma. The bruising to his body had a strong-smelling lotion applied to them and a sedative was administered whilst Hosken was still lying in a dead faint. Angove, armed with a considerable amount of bottles and potions, took charge of the patient who was placed, gently, in the back of the Polmennor cart. Rip lay at his side, giving voice to the occasional mournful whine, but in the main contenting himself with licking the young man's hand.

"I have no sympathy for him, Thomas, for he thought to escape you and run away. His hurts will mend and his scars will fade but in two days time he is to be my husband. Bad enough that my acquaintances say I have bought a man to marry, but now they will imply that he had to be beaten in order that we could tie the knot!" Miss Polmennor almost screamed in temper.

"They will know he was attacked by a vicious traveller, Patience, for the story will soon spread," Angove assured her calmly.

"Oh will they?" she asked, "And pray how will it be explained that this vagabond attacked him. Did he pounce upon him in the street, perchance? For if it was proclaimed that he was found in an alley, surely questions will be asked as to how this...this fool found himself there! Did this ruthless fellow come across Hosken and drag him off when you were looking the other way? I think not!" She gave a sob in frustration, then left the room, slamming the door behind her.

The young man in the bed let out a low groan.

"Oooh!" he moaned, "My head hurts."

Angove crossed to his side and picked up a cloth that was soaking in a bowl of lavender water. He wrung it out and then carefully placed it across Hosken's forehead.

"Is that better, lad?" he asked considerately.

"Yes, yes thank you, Mr Angove," replied Hosken. He groaned again and mentioned that he seemed to ache all over his body.

"You 'ave suffered a severe beating, Hosken, and almost had your throat cut. Lucky for you that assistance arrived when it did," Angove informed him.

"Yes, indeed," confirmed Archelaus, "Please to thank the fellow who saved my life, for I am most beholden to him."

"Wish to thank him do 'ee, Hosken?" asked Thomas with a grin, "I think that can be arranged."

He went to the door, opened it, and in a flash, Rip was in the room. With one leap he jumped onto the bed and stood astride the now terrified young man.

"Don't be afeared, Hosken, for 'tis only your saviour, come to see if you be well again. He has been most concerned for you, whining and carrying on something fierce," Angove told him.

Archelaus blinked in surprise, but Rip, ecstatic to see him awake again, licked his face all over, his tail wagging wildly all the time.

"Saw off your attacker and then stood by to guard you until we got there," Angove told him proudly. "He be some dog, Hosken, to go against a man with a knife the way he did, don't 'ee think?"

The young fellow in the bed would have agreed, but his latest friend refused to give him the opportunity. His continuous licking made it impossible for Hosken to reply, yet he did manage to return Angove's grin, even though the pain in his face caused him to moan once more.

On the morning of the wedding, Henry Rowse drove a dejected individual to the nearby village. With the horse left in the care of a village lad, they walked the short distance to the church, shook hands with the vicar at the door and then moved inside. In a short space of time, a coach bowled up the road and stopped outside of the same church. A small crowd of curious onlookers had gathered to view the proceedings. Thomas Angove, very finely attired, stepped down from the coach. He held out his hand as first his wife and then his daughter alighted. Miss Polmennor was the last to leave, and a revelation she looked. She wore a cream silk dress, trimmed with the finest lace and covered in delicate knots of ribbons, a delightful bonnet, tied with a pink ribbon, covered her hair, and she was adorned in her finest jewels; the effect was quite entrancing and made the little gathering gasp in wonder.

Thomas Angove smiled, held out his arm and together they entered the church, Betty and Cissy Angove following behind them. Henry Rowse, acting as the best man, prodded the groom, who wearily stood to his feet. When his bride arrived at his side, he could not trouble himself to lift his gaze from the floor and throughout the service it was most notable that he seemed to show not the slightest interest in the proceedings. He placed the ring on Miss Polmennor's finger mechanically, and when told that he could now kiss his bride, he did not bother until his wife stamped on his foot to remind him that it was part of the ceremony. Consequently, the lightest touch of his lips briefly brushed her cheek.

They walked down the aisle, arm in arm and stood framed in the doorway. The local people smiled and waved, some even applauded, but the occasion did not seem especially joyous. The groom's demeanour accounted for some of the muted rejoicing, though his appearance certainly added amusement to the sombre event. Mr Hosken wore his finest clothes, yet on his face a cut and swollen lip, a severely bruised cheek and a magnificent black eye were far more entertaining to behold. The bride's expression could best be described as glacial and when the newly married couple got into the coach, it was noted that the bride herself closed the door - so sharply that the horse jumped in its harness.

On arriving back at Bosmenna, the farmhands and the household staff, or those not required in the house, had assembled in the yard. They cheered and whooped when the coach arrived at the steps to the old house. Their appreciation was due to their having been given time off, to partake of a magnificent spread of food that the mistress had arranged to be set out for them in the barn. Planks of wood were set across trestles to serve as tables. White sheets served for tablecloths and plates of every size and description and filled to capacity with a varied assortment of food covered the tables. Large pitchers of ale provided for the workers thirst. Once the obligatory cheering had been completed and the couple had disappeared into the house, the workforce turned as one and ran, in a mad frenzy, for the designated barn. Their mistress was a good employer, but it was not every day that she spent her largesse so freely in order to entertain them.

In the house, the celebrations - if they could be so named - were quiet and restrained. An impressive spread had been set out, yet the married couple scarcely ate a morsel. Mrs Hosken declined sustenance because her day had been ruined by the facial disfigurement of her husband, Mr Hosken felt sick to his soul and had lost his appetite completely. Thomas Angove, holding a full plate in his hand, took the empty seat beside the groom. Rip sat at Hosken's feet, contentedly asleep now that the young man had returned to the house.

"Well, that wasn't so bad, was it Mr Hosken, sir?" he enquired cheerfully. The sudden change in address had no effect on Archelaus at all.

"I imagine everything went as Miss Polmennor wished for it to do," sighed the young man, with disinterest.

Thomas chuckled at his companion's mistake. " 'Tis Mrs Hosken now, sir, she's no longer Miss Polmennor, thanks to you," he corrected him, jovially. Hosken turned his battered face towards him and sighed heavily.

"I think I would rather be swinging from a rope in Bodmin, thank you all the same, Mr Angove," he muttered wearily.

"You call me Angove now, lad, or Thomas, but not Mr Angove. You're my employer now you see," he informed him. Concerned at the young man's train of thought, Angove tried of his best to point out the advantages that were now accruing to him. "You'll have the freedom to roam much more than previously, and if your wife thinks fit, you'll be allowed to visit in the town with friends and…" but here he was interrupted by his companion.

"Friends?" he queried, and pointing to his face said: "this is how my friends have treated me. I've lost my right to be one of them now, Mr Angove. I am as Kelly said I was, merely a puppet. Dressed in the finest with nothing in my pocket. No one wants me now." He gave another heavy sigh, awakening Rip, who yawned and then turned to lick the young man's hand affectionately.

Thomas, saddened by the groom's remarks and not quite sure how to reply, said kindly: "Rip seems to have become most fond of 'ee, sir."

For the first time that day, a glimmer of a smile appeared on the young man's face.

Turning to Thomas, he remarked with a low chuckle: "Unfortunately, I didn't marry the dog, Mr Angove!"

Thomas threw back his head and his booming laugh filled the room. This action did not go unnoticed by Hosken's abandoned spouse.

"Archie!" shrieked the irate lady seated at the head of the table.

At the sound of her voice, the smile disappeared from her husband's face.

"Excuse me, Mr Angove, sir, but I think I hear my beloved calling," and Archelaus got to his feet and trudged towards his wife.

When he reached her, she motioned him to the seat by her side. He sat down heavily and stared at the empty plate set before him.

Smiling at a serving girl who was busily removing some empty glasses, Patience remarked, through gritted teeth: "I never expected to enjoy this day, Archie, but neither did I ever imagine that, in spite of all my plans, you could so effectively have ruined them!"

Archelaus hung his head, having nothing to say.

She took a deep breath in an attempt to control her temper before continuing, with an angry tone to her voice: "Have you seen your face?"

Her husband nodded.

"God alone knows what is being said down in the village and out in the barn!" she snapped, flushing with mortification.

Archelaus sat slumped in his chair, vouchsafing no comment.

After a period of silence, Mrs Hosken cleared her throat and, seemingly absorbed in the arrangement of flowers in the bowl before her, began to speak in a harsh whisper: "When we retire for the night, it will be to separate rooms, do you understand?"

Once again, Hosken nodded his head.

"Should anyone ask, I shall inform them that Dr Simcott advised rest for you because of the recent injuries you have sustained," she told him. "However, when those same injuries have healed, do not expect to be welcomed to my bed, do I make myself clear, Archie?"

"Perfectly," he said woodenly.

"Good!" Patience replied succinctly. This should have been the answer she required, but in some strange way she felt most annoyed. Puzzled at his reaction, she turned her head to study her new husband. He appeared to be completely devoid of any emotion. She would like to have witnessed some sign of regret but none was apparent. Piqued by this, she cleared her throat again.

"This might not always be the case, of course, Archie," she attempted cautiously, but this remark failed to produce a response either.

Blushing fiercely, she smoothed an imaginary crease from the tablecloth with one delicately gloved hand. Thomas Angove had told her earlier that morning, prior to leaving the house, that in his humble opinion, he thought her the prettiest bride in Cornwall. She was aware, having taken a great deal of trouble over her appearance, that she was looking particularly attractive. For her husband to fail even to notice this fact rattled her composure. Of course, she reasoned practically, when she had sought a husband, she had not attempted to find a lover, but some semblance of interest from the man at her side would have been desirable under the circumstances.

Clearing her throat, she was forced into an embarrassing revelation.

"I imagine, after a period of becoming better acquainted, that it will not always be the case for me to retire to my bedchamber alone, Archie," she intimated, two spots of colour prominent on her cheeks.

"Well, let me be the first to congratulate whoever it is that your fancy alights on, ma'am," replied her husband promptly. Then, without waiting for a reply, he got up from his seat, bowed stiffly and, accompanied by the dog, left the room before she had a chance to digest her husbands remark.

CHAPTER 7

"I'm the one to blame, Betty," Thomas Angove told his wife, "so I must do of my best to put matters right between 'em."

"Dussen talk so daft!" his wife scolded him. She busied herself with kneading the dough on her kitchen table.

"No, 'tis true," sighed her husband; "for I chose him to be her husband. I believed he'd be overjoyed to find himself to be so well set-up, but it hasn't happened."

"More fool 'im then," retorted Betty, convinced that her husband could never be at fault.

"Patience is being difficult, so that 'aven't helped matters," he acknowledged woefully.

Placing the dough in a large bowl, putting a cloth over it and leaving it to prove, Betty Angove dusted the flour from her hands. Her brow was creased in thought.

"How don't 'ee take 'en under yer wing, as it were? Take 'en about with 'ee and show 'en how to do things," she suggested. "The mistress will notice, never you fear. If she do see you both going about together I 'speclate she'll be most impressed to see what a high regard you got for 'en."

"Why, missus," cried Thomas, "that's a damn fine idea! I could teach him about the farm and farming. Show him all manner of things. The poor chap is pining away and that's something I hate to see in any man."

"Pining away?" exclaimed Mrs Angove in disbelief, "You should see what he do get through at mealtimes! The mistress could'n 'ave a conversation with 'en if she wanted to, 'cos 'ee be forever eating!"

"I know that! 'Tis the way he do look; never smiling, always moping about, showing no interest in what be going on around him, that's what I mean. Remember when he came here what a jolly, cheeky lad he was?" he remembered with a fond smile. "Patience made sure that side of him disappeared fast nuff!"

"And with good reason!" snapped his wife, "Picking a man out the gutter iddn the best way to find a husband!"

"I think he could be a fine fellow, with a little training and some more time spent about him," remarked her husband in defence. He was determined to prove that he had chosen well, so later that morning he asked Mr Hosken if he would like to learn to shoot a gun.

"I thought perhaps you could go off shooting with me on the farm," he encouraged. "That's a good way to pass an afternoon, you know."

"I know nothing of guns, Mr Angove," replied Archelaus dubiously.

"Come with me, sir. That'll soon be rectified," Thomas told him firmly.

The two men removed to the upper field at the back of the house. The field was of medium size but was notable for the fact that a mound was the most prominent feature at the top of it. This made it an ideal site for shooting practice because the adjacent field sloped away. Consequently, any misfire was unlikely to damage the livestock or any farmhands who might be there when a gun was discharged. Mr Angove, carrying his old flintlock and his leather shooting bag, began to explain the procedure on loading and firing to a somewhat disinterested young man. Standing on the edge of the mound and about fifteen feet from the hedge, Angove took considerable trouble to initiate Archelaus in the complexities of shooting.

"Now, sir, we call this getting the gun primed and ready," he explained enthusiastically. "First, make sure the striker is rotated to here, that's what is called half-cock, now take the powder out of your bag," and he produced a small sealed paper packet from the leather bag that he had strung over his shoulder, "and rip the top off the packet with your teeth." Hosken watched him as he spat out a small piece of paper, "place a bit of powder in this bit, which is called the pan," he continued, "and then put the cover over it. You following this, Mr Hosken?"

The young man nodded but did not seem to be very impressed with the proceedings. Undaunted, a determined Mr Angove continued with his explanation: "Pour the rest of the powder down the barrel, or muzzle, as we do call it, then take out the ball," and he produced a small ball of lead from the bag. "Wrap the paper that was holding the powder round it and using this rod here..." here he removed the rod from the underside of the gun and inserted it into the end of the muzzle, "...and push the ball down the barrel." He used the rod to ram the contents into the bottom end.

"Now, take the gun in your hands," he said, passing it to Archelaus, who staggered under the weight.

"It's very heavy, Mr Angove, sir!"

Thomas sighed in frustration but continued with determination.

"Now, see that broken branch that's dangling off the hawthorn tree there?" he asked.

"Yes sir," replied his pupil.

"Well, aim your gun at that!"

Archelaus did as he was instructed, his face going slightly pink with the strain of holding the weight of the gun.

"Bring the striker to full-cock, Mr Hosken," instructed Angove. At this point Hosken pointed out that he had not been shown how to do that, so Angove took a deep breath and explained the procedure.

"Now, line up the barrel of the gun on that branch, Mr Hosken, sir and gently...gently now, squeeze the trigger," he advised, biting his lip in anticipation.

There was a slight sound as the flint hit the frizzen, followed by an extremely loud bang.

Mr Angove, peering through a cloud of smoke left by the discharge of the powder, suddenly leapt into the air with glee. "You did it, sir, you hit it!" he cried in delight, pointing to the hawthorn tree from which the remnants of a shattered branch dangled. He turned to slap his student on the back in congratulation, but discovered to his dismay that the young man was nowhere to be seen. The gun, still smoking, lay on the ground, but Hosken seemed to have completely disappeared.

A groan coming from the field behind him made him look over the edge of the mound, and directly behind his firing position, face-upwards in the grass lay Archelaus Hosken, blinking in surprise.

"What happened?" he gasped.

Mr Angove ran down the slope and, bending down to help him to his feet, apologised profusely. "I'm some sorry, sir, I forgot tell 'ee about the recoil. I should have told you to lean into it like this," and he demonstrated the action of a man leaning slightly forward whilst holding an imaginary gun in his hand. "See, when you do fire a gun, the force of the explosion…"

But Archelaus, rubbing his bruised shoulder, interrupted to inform him that he thought he would not like to fire a gun very much.

"We could get one made to your weight, sir," advised Angove anxiously, but the young man shook his head.

"I don't think I want to be deafened and to stand a chance of breaking my shoulder, just to fire a gun, thank you, Mr Angove," he informed his tutor, and turning on his heel made his way slowly back to the house, rubbing the top of his arm all the while.

Before the end of the week, Mr Angove formed another plan and advised Mr Hosken that he was to go on a fishing expedition in a local fisherman's boat.

"A boat?" asked Archelaus, with some trepidation, "I don't know about that, Mr Angove, sir, for I have never been in a boat."

"Nothing to worry about, sir," said Thomas, breezily, "You'll soon find your sea legs."

Convinced that the young man would enjoy the experience, they set out in the afternoon for their seafaring trip. They had scarcely left the little harbour before Archelaus began to turn green in the face, within a mile of the shore he had lost his lunch over the side and before they had gone another mile, his breakfast was to follow. Mr Angove, disappointed by the turn of events and concerned that the young fellow was looking none too well, advised the grinning seaman to return to Lamorna because it was obvious that his charge was not enjoying the experience.

Archelaus, sick and soaked with salt water, climbed into the cart and waited dejectedly to be transported back to Bosmenna. Mr Angove, feeling guilty and saddened by the turn of events, felt that they should visit a local hostelry on the way home. He considered that some alcohol would restore the fellow, for he still looked most pale.

In hindsight, Mr Angove had to admit that to encourage the young man to imbibe potent amounts of brandy was not the cleverest of actions to follow when the gentlemen in question had nothing left in his stomach with which to absorb the drink.

Thomas returned with his charge, almost half an hour after the dining hour was due to begin. Patience, a creature of habit, was not best pleased to be kept waiting.

However, when Angove propped her somewhat incoherent husband in his chair it was to be noted that the smile had returned to his face. It was not his former cheeky grin however, more an alcoholic smirk that lay across his features.

"I have been drinking," Archelaus informed his wife, and then hiccupped.

"So I see!" snapped his fuming wife, and then berated Thomas for allowing her husband to get himself into such a state.

Angove apologised profusely and admitted that he did not realise that the drink would affect her spouse so badly.

"I thought that, he having been so ill on the boat, a few drinks would help to restore him," he explained apologetically.

"Restore him to what?" questioned an irate Mrs Hosken; "and I'm not sure how you would define 'a few drinks', Angove!"

Thomas hung his head in shame, and could do no more than apologise once more for his stupidity. His wife, Betty, flashed him a look that did not augur well for his next conversation with her.

Archelaus, now lolling in his chair, smiled inanely at his wife and told her that she was looking most beautiful.

There was a stunned silence.

"What did you say?" asked his shocked wife.

"I said..." and he hiccupped again, "I...I said that you are looking mos...most booful!"

"Must you needs be intoxicated afore you say such words to me, Archie?" she asked, annoyed that he should offer endearments when he was too inebriated to know what he was saying.

"No," confirmed the continuously smiling drunk, "but it helps!" He hiccupped again and announced to Mrs Angove that he would like an extra slice of beef, if that was acceptable, before his legs gave way completely and he slipped off the chair and slid under the dining table. Within a short space of time, loud snores began to echo around the room.

"Damn the man!" screamed his wife, almost hysterical with anger. Rising from her chair, she threw down her napkin and ran from the room, sobbing with rage.

CHAPTER 8

THE consequences of Mr Hosken becoming intoxicated and the effect that this produced on two sets of wives, caused Thomas Angove and Archelaus Hosken to draw closer together in friendship.

Late the following morning, they were sitting together on a hedge, seemingly surveying the cattle in the next field.

"I'm sorry, Mr Hosken, sir. I'd no idea the drink would affect 'ee so badly," apologised Mr Angove.

"No matter, Mr Angove, sir," replied Archelaus wearily.

"Did Patience…I mean, did Mrs Hosken have…um…have much to say to you at the breakfast table, sir?" he enquired, purposely avoiding the young man's eye.

"Quite a bit," said Hosken, nodding his head, and then added: "She is a remarkable woman, for she appeared not to be lost for words. I thought she would run out of things to call me, but that didn't seem to be the case." He turned to Mr Angove and asked, on a sudden thought: "Are all wives like that, sir? I only ask because I have never had one before."

Thomas nodded glumly, for since returning with his employer's inebriated husband the previous night, his wife had let it be known of her own poor opinion of her spouse in much the same manner.

They sat in silence surveying the scene before them. Mr Angove had not given up in his attempts to involve his young charge in some form of activity, either on the farm or in the locality, but he thought it best to curtail any activities for the present time.

When the lunch hour arrived they returned to the house together, Angove to make his way to the kitchen and Hosken to the dining room. Neither expected to enjoy the experience so when they arrived in the hallway, they turned towards each other, shook hands and wished each other good luck, as if it was the most natural thing to do. In both cases, each man understood the predicament of the other, and sympathised with his respective position.

However, with his determination undimmed, Thomas Angove succeeded in getting the newly married Mr Hosken to take some interest in the farm. Admittedly, Archelaus Hosken, although travelling the country for nearly all of his life, found it difficult to have to stay in one place, but circumstances had finally made him understand that he had little choice in the matter. He had tried to escape, but with Kelly's attack had come the realization that his former life was lost to him. He could not rejoin a group of travellers, for they no longer considered that he was a part of their community. The local populace viewed him with distaste; to them he was an untrustworthy person and not the sort of neighbour with whom they wished to have any dealings. For the most part, his wife treated him with cold disdain, so he fell into the habit of supplying monosyllabic answers to her questions. This seemed to annoy her for some reason, but as he tried for the most part to avoid her company he found the situation bearable by spending his time with Mr Angove whenever possible. Thomas strove to improve Hosken's reading, writing and mathematical skills as well. The latter ability Archelaus found difficult to master because he was not always correct at recognising the figures when they were written down. However, even this skill improved over time, so that it was only when presented with a large number of figures that the young man became confused as to their true worth.

Farming was not a life that Archelaus thought would hold any interest for him, but gradually the turn of the season brought with it new experiences. He became physically fitter with every passing day, due in the main to having a plentiful supply of food to eat for the first time in his life. The young man was of medium height and could not perform some of the tasks that the taller, but more muscular Angove, could accomplish with ease. However, Thomas encouraged him to attempt far more than he thought himself capable of and in some strange way that he could not comprehend, Archelaus began to enjoy the whole experience. He spent his days in Mr Angove's company, being taught a multitude of skills, some of which he mastered easily and others that he was not so successful in accomplishing. However, Thomas was pleased that his employer began to show some enthusiasm for his new situation. Unfortunately, he was dejected over the state of the relationship that existed between the master and mistress. They appeared to be as distant from each other as ever, and apart from dining together and attending church in each others company neither seemed to wish for their relationship to be placed on a friendlier footing. Angove, the eternal optimist, determined that this situation could not be allowed to continue.

Each year, a harvest supper was arranged for the workers and, as on the wedding day, the barn was used to house the occasion. However, this time a place was set for Mr Hosken at the head of the table. More in hope than expectation, Mr Angove arranged for a seat to be left for Mrs Hosken at the opposite end, should she wish to grace the proceedings. It was not Patience's usual habit to attend the supper; she provided the food, but because of her aloof nature, she would not naturally mix with her workforce. Her husband, on the other hand, having been taken under Angove's wing and thrown in amongst the labourers on the farm, knew them all on first name terms and enjoyed their company. Archelaus looked forward to the feast with excited anticipation, fully expecting to enjoy it just as much as the workhands.

It was a considerable surprise to discover that, just as the meal began, Mrs Hosken marched through the open door, sat herself at the seat reserved for her and smiled, rather brightly, upon the proceedings. From the other end of the table, her husband regarded her with a rather wary expression on his face, but Angove, knowing Patience as he did, determined that her presence would not place a damper on the event. The natural exuberance of Bosmenna's workforce carried the day, though in the beginning their speech was a trifle restrained. However, the copious amounts of ale that they consumed meant that the supper soon became a rather boisterous event. Henry Rowse sang a song and they all joined in the chorus, including Mr Hosken, Matty Tregonning gave them a tune on his fiddle, managing to master most of the notes in spite of consuming rather too much ale, others of the workforce paired up and began to dance around the table.

Patience watched in wonder at the transformation that came over her restrained husband; he danced with Lily the milkmaid,

Cissy Angove and even Mrs Angove. He joined the men in a resounding rendition of Hearts of Oak, juggled some apples from the bowl, much to the workforce's appreciation, and seemed to be enjoying himself wholeheartedly. The smile was back on his face and the twinkle in his eye, she noted, just as it had been when she had removed him from the lock-up.

"Mrs 'Osken, would 'ee like to sing fer we?" asked Henry Rowse, grinning happily.

"Well...I...I," stammered Patience, taken aback to be asked to perform.

A silence fell over the table and all eyes were directed towards her. For a moment, she looked unsure as to how to continue. Archelaus, studying her features, asked Tregonning for the fiddle. Re-tuning it slightly, he then began to play Greensleeves, much more tunefully that Tregonning had shown himself capable of and much to the appreciation of the assembled crowd.

Patience, blushing rosily and mightily confused by the turn of events, missed her cue to begin. Her husband played the introduction again and, looking directly into her eyes, nodded his head to indicate when she should start to sing. She began nervously but, emboldened by the smiling faces regarding her, she soon got into her stride. When she finished, it was to thunderous cheers of appreciation and she bowed her head and expressed her thanks, a delightful smile brightening her normally stern countenance. She lifted her glowing face and caught her husband's eye, he inclined his head, but she detected no hint of a smile on his lips. Disconcerted by this, for she thought he would have been more demonstrative, she smiled upon him in a more loving way than she had ever done before. The effect was not what she expected at all, her husband turning away to pass the fiddle back to Matty, asked him to play a jig and, pulling Lily towards him, demanded that the 'Lady Lily', as he called her, should honour him with another dance. Thomas Angove, realising that Hosken's actions were not being appreciated by the young man's spouse, sprang to his feet immediately and asked Mrs Hosken to dance with him. Patience, not wishing to lose face in front of such a knowing crowd, accepted with alacrity, more to cover her confusion at the rebuttal she had just received than to demonstrate her dancing ability.

The evening was most convivial, for all but one of the participants. Patience Hosken drank scarcely anything at all and had to make her way back to her house alone. Her husband, on the other hand, had seemed incapable of resisting the ale that had been placed on the table. By the time she left the barn, she had been made aware of two facts: the first was that her husband had been accepted by his workforce and had become a respected member of it, and the second was that he had preferred the comforts of drink to having to spend his time with her. In the doorway, she turned and looked back, a mixture of annoyance and regret upon her face. On a mound of hay in the corner of the barn, Henry Rowse, Matthew Tregonning and her husband lay, snoring in unison, oblivious to their surroundings. At Hosken's feet lay Rip, as full of scraps of discarded food as his belly could contain. Brightly, Patience called the dog to her, but he only raised his head for a moment, wagged his tail briefly, and then returned to his interrupted sleep, his chin resting happily on her husband's foot. It was extremely lowering for her to understand that her position as head of the household had shifted unknowingly to rest upon her husband's shoulders. It was also a fact that annoyed her greatly and did not bode well for her husband's appearance at the breakfast table on the morrow.

"I have no sympathy, Archie, for in my opinion you have brought this upon yourself," snapped Patience Hosken.

The recipient of this remark sat opposite to her, at the other end of the dining table, holding his head in his hands. Archelaus Hosken had never been a master of alcohol and, even in his previous life, had rarely drunk to excess. However, last night he had determined to enjoy the occasion and had joined in the festivities amongst his newly acquired group of friends with gusto. He thought that the presence of his wife would sour the event, but he was determined that this would not be the case. If it required that he should drink rather more than he would normally do, than so be it. His head ached abominably, but the evening was most enjoyable and he was prepared to suffer the consequences.

"You danced with Lily Tonkin twice!" she cried, her cheeks flushed.

"Yes, my dear," he replied wearily.

"I supposed you enjoyed her company!"

"Yes, my dear."

A plate rattled at the end of the table, but with his eyes not wishing to be stabbed by the light flooding into the room, he continued to hide his head.

"Why?"

"Pardon?"

"Why? Why dance with her?" screamed his wife, her voice rising in pitch with each question.

Archelaus considered carefully and then pronounced, with a smile on his lips, "She has the most beautiful complexion." He raised his head at that moment and his eyes widened in alarm as he espied an airborne plate advancing on his position. Quickly and painfully, he ducked his head beneath the table as the flying crockery missed him by mere inches, smashing into the wall at the end of the room. Rip barked in confusion and moved closer to his master.

"How dare you!" shouted Patience, white hot with fury.

Mrs Angove, biting her lip to trap her smile, walked across the room and bent down to pick up the shards. Placing them in her apron, she turned and went back to the door. Asking to be excused, she left the room, closing the door carefully behind her. In the dining room, Hosken and his wife heard only the sound of her raucous laughter echoing along the hall as she made her way to the kitchen.

"See what you have done?" screamed his wife, pointing to the door. "You have connived to make me look a fool!"

"No, my dear," he offered faintly, and then added, incautiously; "I think you did that all by yourself."

His wife shrieked in temper, even to a man not suffering the effects of too much alcohol the sound would have been unnerving. When he noted that his wife's hand was searching for another piece of crockery, he threw caution to the wind, left his seat with alacrity and bolted for the door. Another plate broke upon the solid oak and the pieces fell to the ground, but by this time Hosken and Rip were safe in the hall. Archelaus considered that it would be far safer to forego his breakfast on this occasion and set off to discover the whereabouts of Thomas Angove. Rip followed faithfully at his feet, even he somewhat bemused by the unwarranted behaviour of his mistress.

CHAPTER 9

THERE was to be a horse fair on the following Wednesday, after the harvest supper. Upon giving the matter some thought, Thomas approached his mistress to enquire about having some time off to attend. He considered it to be a wise move to acquire an exceptionally fine mare that he knew was to be offered for auction that day. However, Mrs Hosken seemed not to be as interested in the farm as previously, so he asked his employer if she would wish to attend.

"Not particularly," she told him abruptly, and continued to flip the pages of the book she was perusing in a distracted manner.

"Take Archie, instead," she said eventually. "Perhaps if he is seen to be accompanying you it will be noted by the local populace that he is more to be trusted. After the way he was treated by the travellers he encountered the last time, I doubt he will be so keen to abscond!"

"That's a fine idea, Patience, for I have often thought he should be encouraged to go about some more," responded Angove, but added that if the two of them were to be seen together it might look the more fitting.

Two dark, angry eyes fixed themselves on his face. "You may not be aware of it, Thomas, but my husband does not show any desire for my company," she snapped.

"I have told you before, Patience, that if you were to show some…um…interest in Archie, then…" but his speech was curtailed when Mrs Hosken shut her book with a snap.

"Interest in that useless vagabond? I most certainly will not!" she shouted, and getting up from her chair, she flounced from the room, slamming the door behind her.

Thomas sighed, shrugged his shoulders, and went off to find Mr Hosken.

When he told the young man of his proposed visit to the fair, Archelaus looked most concerned, but Angove pointed out: "You have only to stay by my side and you will have no problems. After all, your last encounter was due mainly to your desire to leave my company," he pointed out wisely, "Don't feel that way now, do 'ee?"

Hosken grinned and shook his head. Before his marriage, he had felt that his life was doomed to despair, but he had to acknowledge that Thomas Angove had worked hard to make him a part of the life of the farm. He appreciated the efforts that had been made on his behalf and had come to think upon the man as a valued friend.

"Do 'ee know much about horses, Mr Hosken, sir?" asked Angove, as they walked across the field to the spot where the horse sales were being held. Archelaus thought for a moment, then informed him that he had an average knowledge, nothing more.

"Well, you'll have a chance to learn some more today, won't 'ee, sir?"

"Yes, Mr Angove, I will," replied his protégé, keeping a wary eye on a group of travellers standing to the edge of the main crowd. He recognised some of them but they made no attempt to communicate with him. Time had shifted his perspective, he observed, for now he had no wish to be part of their fraternity. His rejection by Kelly, and the manner of it, had taught him that his present course was the one he had to follow, and that his past had been lost to him forever.

It was during the course of the auction, that Thomas Angove was to discover that his employer, though displaying no more than an average knowledge of horseflesh, had an uncanny ability to predict who would make the final bid in each of the sales. On being asked how he had come by this talent, Archelaus pointed out - with some discomfort – that, as a thief, he had to be aware of the character of the people from whom he was trying to steal.

"Some of them can spot what you are about in a minute, Mr Angove. Others, like yourself, are more aware of what is going on around them," he explained, "but you have to have a knowledge of what people understand of certain situations. They act in a different way, you see. If I am trying to get someone to purchase an item from me I study that person most closely, to see if I can get him to the point where he will buy the moon from me if I should offer to sell it. Others will not be drawn, no matter how persuasive you try to be, so you have to know at what price to withdraw the offer. That way you stand a better chance of a sale. Many a time, I've seen an old widow march proudly away with a fine item of jewellery that I have offered for sale for little more than the price of a jug of ale! A similar object sold to a blushing damsel, who I have praised and charmed, would net me a fine return," he turned his head and studied his friend sadly. "When all is said and done, Mr Angove, sir, 'tis not the most creditable of traits to have to your name," he concluded.

"You may think so, Mr Hosken, sir, but it may prove invaluable to me today," Thomas said sagely. They moved to the front of the crowd to get a better view of the horses and for Mr Hosken to be able to see the faces of the other bidders. When the mare that interested Thomas was brought out, the faces of many of the men showed an interest in the beast, but one man in particular seemed intent on staring at the Bosmenna party instead.

Richard Polmennor had no desire to purchase the animal, but he could not resist to thwart Mr Angove's attempts to buy the mare for his cousin. The animal was too small to carry his son or himself and his wife had never learnt to ride, so it would serve no useful purpose to buy it, but he had some money at his disposal and he determined that his cousin would not be given the pleasure of owning the beast without paying a small fortune for it. He knew he could run Angove to a high price for he had done it before. 'You'll pay for this beauty, Patience,' he thought to himself and a smirk quivered on his lip.

Across from him, Archelaus Hosken caught Polmennor's eye and, doffing his cap, bowed politely. Polmennor merely glared angrily at him in return.

"Don't be the first to bid, Mr Angove," hissed Archelaus, out of the corner of his mouth. Thomas, a fine judge of horseflesh, whispered back: "But I am most wishful to purchase the mare, Mr Hosken, sir, and I would not miss my chance."

"You will purchase it, Mr Angove," whispered the young man in return, his eye viewing the crowd before him, "but I sincerely hope that it will not be at the price Mr. Polmennor would like you to pay!"

The bidding commenced and stayed at a low amount, the seller shaking his head at the auctioneer with every bid declared. Hosken, seemingly bored by the whole proceedings, did not look at the mare at all. He seemed to wish himself a mile away, so uninterested did he look.

Slowly, the amounts offered crept upwards and the seller's expression began to look more hopeful. Finally, only Polmennor and Angove were making any bids for the animal, the others assembled had no interest in the beast for, although the mare would make a fine riding horse, they wanted only a creature that could be of more use about their farms.

"Top the last bid, Mr Angove, but not by much," whispered Archelaus, brushing some dust from his sleeve.

Mr. Angove did as he was instructed. For this beast he was prepared to pay a hundred guineas, for he considered the mare a most rare and fine animal and had told Archelaus that he would be prepared to pay that figure. Hosken, viewing the actions of the seller, considered that he would accept a far lower sum. However, it was the expression on the face of Richard Polmennor that interested him the more. Gradually, the figure for the animal increased until Thomas Angove, following the instructions of his employer, offered the sum of fifty guineas.

"Now bite your lip, Mr Angove, and start to look worried," Hosken hissed to his companion.

Polmennor, seeing the look on the other man's face, could not contain the smile on his own from spreading.

"Sixty guineas, sir!" he shouted to the auctioneer, who almost dropped his gavel in surprise at the sudden rise in the amount offered. A gasp was heard from the crowd.

Thomas, his heart racing, was about to open his mouth when to his amazement he heard his companion say: "Keep your mouth shut, sir. Bowing your head in despair would be a useful action, as well."

Angove obliged, but he wanted the mare so badly, his hand itched to signal another offer. He was prepared to pay the price he had set himself after all and Hosken knew it.

Polmennor, seeing Thomas Angove's submission of defeat, laughed aloud and turned from the ring, delighted with his ploy.

His farm manager could see to the details and the auctioneer was well aware of what Polmennor was trying to do, indeed, of that which he had succeeded in doing. Of course, Polmennor admitted to himself, the mare was of no use, and with the exception of his cousin he could think of no other in the locality that would wish to acquire it, but it mattered not a jot. He had trumped the Bosmenna group and he could hardly contain his glee.

"Sixty guineas, going once, gentlemen," sang out the auctioneer.

Hosken's hand shot out and grabbed Angove by the arm and Thomas turned on him with fury. "Wait!" instructed Archelaus fiercely.

Hosken watched as Polmennor continued to walk away from the scene, swaggering as he did so.

Angove was forbidden to raise his hand at the second request and Archelaus noted that by this time Polmennor was a considerable distance from the auction, but still he waited. "Will you fund me, Mr Angove?" he hissed quietly, his eye still on his wife's cousin.

Startled, Thomas told him that he would.

"Going…going…" intoned the auctioneer, when he noted another hand had been raised.

"Sixty-one guineas," offered Archelaus boldly.

"Sixty-one guineas, new bidder," was proclaimed. Polmennor turned, but Angove, standing head and shoulders above the crowd, still stood with his head down, a most dejected look on his face. Polmennor's own farm manager, Mr Symons, broke from the ring of people and started to call to his employer, gesticulating wildly.

"New bidder, eh?" surmised Richard, and then grinned, pleased to think that he would not have to pay for the useless animal after all. It did not matter to him who bought the wretched animal; if he had been willing to pay, Angove could have purchased it. He turned and continued to walk away, laughing to himself as he did so, but stopped immediately when the auctioneer intoned.

"Sold to Mr Archelaus Hosken at sixty-one guineas, gentlemen!"

He turned, a look of thunderstruck amazement across his features, to see Mr Hosken having his hand shaken enthusiastically by Thomas Angove. The thunderous look on Polmennor's face was not improved when Archelaus made him another bow, doffing his hat once more, though this time he appeared to be laughing at him.

"Damn you, Hosken," ranted Polmennor to the wind, "I'll bring you down for this!"

CHAPTER 10

WHEN the mare arrived, along with Thomas and Archelaus, in the yard at Bosmenna, Patience could not hide her delight. She loved to ride and thought her latest acquisition a delight to behold. When told the tale of the auction, she smiled upon her husband. Though he noted her expression, he turned away and headed towards the fields where he knew he would find Lily, employed in her milking duties. An angry frown crossed Mrs Hosken's face as she saw her husband go through the yard gate and head towards the small meadow where the milkmaid would be at work.

Within ten minutes, he returned, walking towards Mr Angove, who was watching as his employer had the horse led up and down by a stable lad so that Patience could see it go through its paces.

"Well, Patience?" queried Thomas, with a smile.

"A fine creature, Thomas," she replied, enthusiastically, her eye catching sight of her husband.

"You have bought a fine animal here, Archie," she told him, trying not to seem ungrateful, although she felt slighted that her husband should wish to visit with the milkmaid quite so blatantly.

"Thank you," he replied and bowed stiffly.

"And that's not all he bought," announced Thomas with a grin. "For he asked to borrow some money to purchase ribbons from a stall." Mr Angove had provided the money with a good heart, for he had assumed that his friend wanted to buy some small trifle for his wife. Considering the cold relations that existed between the young couple, he imagined that Archie's actions would be well thought of, even by one as glacial as Patience could be.

"Ribbons!" exclaimed Mrs Hosken, a surprised smile on her lips. "Did you buy me ribbons, Archie?"

A bright red flush stole across her husband's face. Taking a deep breath, he answered: "No, I did not buy any for you."

In a moment, Patience's features hardened into stone.

"Then for whom have you bought them?" she asked angrily.

Archie gulped but continued bravely, "Lily," he offered in a soft voice.

"Lily!" cried his wife in fury. "You have bought a gift for a milkmaid! How dare you stand before me and tell me such a thing!" Furious, she turned on her heel and ran towards the house.

Thomas turned to his companion and apologised, stiffly, for mentioning the matter. "I thought you had bought them for your wife, sir" he explained, a perplexed look in his eyes.

Hosken held out his hand, in the palm of which lay two pennies. "Lily asked if I could purchase some ribbons for her," he explained to Angove, "and when she saw them just now she gave me the money there and then. So I am returning your loan, Mr Angove, sir," he said simply, and with a brief word of thanks he sighed, trudged up the steps and into the house.

At the dinner hour that evening the meal was conducted in complete silence. Archelaus found himself the recipient of a great number of icy stares, but endeavoured to keep his eyes lowered for the most part. Finally, when Patience had finished eating, Mrs Angove was ordered to return to the kitchen until such time as her services were required.

Archelaus discovered that his appetite had suddenly deserted him and waited at the end of the table in some trepidation.

Watching his wife covertly, he noticed that she threw her napkin down and was not looking altogether pleased to be in his company.

"You may, if you wish, find yourself a companion with whom to spend the night, Archie, but it will not be one of my workers!" she announced in a tight voice. "Is that understood?"

"Yes, my dear," he returned.

"I will not have my milkmaid flaunted before me as your paramour, do you understand?"

"Yes, my dear," he answered, in a subdued tone.

Breathing heavily, Patience demanded to know if he had anything that he wished to say on his behalf. She ranted on at him, becoming more irate with every word she uttered. "No matter what I have to say to you, I receive always the same answers. Have you nothing to say in your defence, Archie?" Hoping for some explanation from her husband, she waited in simmering anger. If only the man would tell her that Lily meant nothing to him, even that he sought her company out of loneliness. An apology, a word of regret, anything would be better than the daily indifference that she suffered.

Archelaus stared at his half-full plate, turning over in his mind the words that he knew he ought to utter. He should explain that Patience was suffering from a misconception and that he had purchased Lily's ribbons at her request because the milkmaid had wanted to adorn her best dress to impress her beau, a stable lad on a local farm. But there was something about his wife that intimidated him and he felt compelled to keep silent. From the day he had entered the premises, she had always the upper hand with him and if he tried to please her, she had no praise for him. Thomas had told him that she was impressed with the way he had learnt to read and write, and acknowledged that he tried of his best to learn about farming. She recognised that, with the opportunities he had been given, he had learnt to make the best of himself, keeping himself clean and tidy and always being mannerly when in company. All manner of things that he had no knowledge of before, he had absorbed and learnt from, yet no words of respect came from his wife's lips. Convincing himself that their lives together must inevitably follow the same relentless pattern, he had subdued his natural exuberance when around her. When on the farm with the workmen, he laughed and joked; with Thomas, he had developed a firm friendship that he had found with no other man in his life before. Not wishing to lose any of the benefits that had accrued to him, he desired only to placate his wife and tried of his best not to annoy her. The latter he found the hardest to accomplish, for it appeared to be the easiest thing of all to turn the woman who sat opposite him into a raging demon. So he sat mute, struggling to find the words.

"Well?" screamed his wife, infuriated by his prolonged silence. "Have you anything to tell me?"

"No, my dear," offered her husband, in hardly more than a whisper.

He prepared himself to duck any missile that would be thrown in his direction, but to his surprise nothing appeared. His wife merely sat at the end of the table, regarding him with despair. Slowly, two tears ran down her cheeks and she began to sob quietly. Unsure what action to follow, Archelaus slowly got up from the table, bowed stiffly and wished her goodnight. Then he strode across the room and let himself out into the hallway. Rip plodded by his side, raising his head, he licked Hosken's hand consolingly.

"Thanks, old fellow," remarked his companion, sadly. "Glad I am to know someone in the house likes my company."

Although Mrs Hosken felt unable to express her appreciation of her husband's accomplishment in out-bidding her neighbour, word soon spread around the locality. It soon became apparent when several neighbouring farmers, always accompanied by their wives, began to call. They made many and varied excuses as to why they had been unable to attend upon the Hoskens before, but it was noted that the young man's success at the auction had impressed all of the local farmers and quite a few of them enjoyed the joke at Richard Polmennor's expense. The gentleman in question realised that his position in the hierarchy of the farming fraternity had caused a shift in favour of the occupants of Bosmenna; he was even less pleased at this unlooked for turn of events.

When his own son, Jasper, expressed a wish to visit with his cousin and his new friend, Archie, Richard Polmennor became most red in the face. He was about to shout his son into submission by threatening to have him committed, when a solution to his problem occurred to him.

"By all means, Jasper. Visit them if you will, for I have business in St. Ives to which I have to attend," he said with a grim smile.

"Oh, thank you father," beamed his son, forgiving and forgetting all the insults he had received on previous occasions when he had asked to visit Bosmenna. In Jasper's innocent mind it meant only that he was allowed to have the couple for his friends. It also meant that he would be able to see Cissy. He smiled happily to himself, for he wished to do that very much indeed.

Jasper was greeted with great delight by the Hoskens, though, familiar as he was to the slights and insults of his own father, he noted immediately that his cousin Patience spoke quite sharply with her husband. He thought that a great shame, for he liked Archie and wanted him to be happy. Jasper was allowed to go and talk with Cissy, too. Archie noted that she was walking towards the field with a large bowl in her hands to hang out some washing, and said: "Why don't you help her, Jasper, because it looks as if that washing is quite heavy."

Putting down his plate with the half eaten cake on it, Jasper stared at them, his mouth hanging open in astonishment, "May I?" he asked in disbelief.

His cousin smiled and nodded her head and the young man needed no second telling. The next moment they heard him running through the hallway calling out: "Cissy! Cissy! Let me help you. The washing is heavy, Cissy!"

"That was a kind thought, Archie," said his wife reasonably.

"He likes Cissy and she likes him," advised her husband.

"I doubt that Cousin Richard will ever allow them to marry. He was determined that Jasper become my husband, to bring the farms together, and when I…when I would not oblige, he was most aggrieved," she said, studying her husband's expression as she spoke.

"He will be a good and loving husband to a woman kind enough to take him on," Archelaus remarked, a soft smile on his face.

"Will you be a good and loving husband, Archie?" she mused.

"Pardon?" asked her husband, taken aback by the question.

"Do you intend to be a good and loving husband, Archie?" she asked again, and stared at him intently.

He was silent for a long while, then raised his head and looked her in the eye, his expression blank and his eyes hard.

"I am as you always wanted me to be, my dear, a name on a piece of paper," he replied evenly.

CHAPTER 11

"My dear," warbled Mrs Prouse, enthusiastically, "He is so charming and obliging. Not like that old fool Dr Simcott!" She smiled at Mrs Hosken and then sipped her tea, noting that Mr Hosken appeared to show interest in the conversation, judging by the polite expression on his face. Not the most handsome of men, she observed, but she was impressed with his charm and manners. This was her first visit alone to Bosmenna and she was amazed that Mr Hosken had been polite enough to sit with them whilst they took tea. Her own spouse would have found an excuse to leave the women together at the first opportunity, for he detested 'nattering women', as he called them. Mrs Hosken's husband had been most mannerly, even getting up and offering her a cake from the plate. 'Mr Prouse will hear of this,' she told herself. Of ample proportions, Mrs Prouse did not need to fill her plate with food, for it was most apparent that the woman ate adequately, but she enjoyed to eat and took advantage of every opportunity that was offered to her.

"I see no reason to change my allegiance from Dr Simcott, Mrs Prouse, for he has always been more than adequate for my needs," replied Patience Hosken serenely.

"But, my dear, he is so old! And now that you are married you may require someone who is more advanced in medical practice." She then proceeded to recount the many times that she had concluded Dr Simcott had not performed his duties adequately.

Mrs Hosken replied that she still held in her belief of the good doctor's abilities.

"Well, when the children start to come along, my dear, you may change your mind!" replied Mrs Prouse sharply, "for as the mother of fourteen, I can assure you that Simcott has very little idea of how his patient wishes to be treated in such a situation. To be told that 'yelling', as he puts it, will not bring the baby into the world the sooner is hardly what one wants to hear at such a time!"

As she was busily engaged in adding another slice of buttered bread to her plate at that moment, she was blissfully unaware of the beetroot flushes that enveloped the faces of the young couple in the room.

Patience, too confused to speak, was relieved to hear her husband's voice ask, after a moment's hesitation, if Mrs Prouse thought the weather would improve, for the almost continuous rain was so depressing, did she not think?

"Oh I so agree, Mr Hosken, for I have ruined two of my best pairs of shoes in spite of wearing pattens! Have you seen the mud in Penzance? My dear, the town is positively awash with the stuff!" She then explained how she had demanded that the town officials should do something about it.

As she prattled on, Patience shot her husband a look of gratitude, but he merely bowed his head by way of acknowledgement and then turned his attention to their guest. If his smile appeared a trifle fixed it was understandable; Mrs Prouse was renowned for the ability to speak on any subject, even if she knew nothing about it, and, regrettably, at great length.

Unfortunately, Mrs Prouse was determined to praise her latest discovery and soon returned to talking of medical matters.

"My dear, I had a boil the size of a teapot! I cannot tell you where, for I should blush to mention it, but Dr Abernathy was politeness itself when he treated me. 'Dear lady' he said, and he has the most divine tone, Mrs Hosken, absolutely divine," trilled Mrs Prouse. "And even when he lanced it, which was excruciatingly painful, I can assure you, and I suffered greatly because of it - my dear, I could not sit for a week! Where was I? Oh yes. Naturally I was most embarrassed at my situation, but he told me: 'Dear lady, I have seen many in my time, but none so exquisite as this.' Well, I felt myself improving from that very moment," she concluded proudly.

Patience heard a suppressed snort of laughter from her husband and flashed him a look to warn him not to give way to his mirth. The twinkling eyes that glanced back at her made her heart contract, but her guest's voice broke the spell.

"Did you speak, Mr Hosken?" snapped Mrs Prouse, reprovingly.

"Do forgive me, ma'am," he replied sweetly, "but I believe I have the beginnings of a cold and I was attempting not to sneeze."

Instantly diverted, Mrs Prouse advised on the many medicaments that she had administered over the years to her own brood, finishing her speech with the information that: "A mustard bath is most efficacious you know. Although, regrettably, Mr Prouse swears by brandy and hot water as the more effective. I shall never understand the desire of the male of the species for intoxicating beverages. At the slightest problem that arises, my husband will immediately pour himself a glass of something. It is so annoying when you are trying to converse with him on a matter of great importance, you know. Frequently, I have found him and - it pains me to say it, Mrs Hosken - in a state of great befuddlement. I am sure you have never had to suffer such a mortifying experience from your dear husband."

She inclined her head and smiled at Mr Hosken condescendingly. He smiled back, but his wife sat with two red spots glowing on her cheeks.

After what seemed like an eternity, Mrs Prouse rose to go, informing them that she hoped that they would visit with her in the not too distant future.

"Now remember, you must call upon me soon. I'm sure we will find so much to talk about," she enthused as she stood outside the house before turning to get into her carriage. This required great efforts on the part of her coachman as Mrs Prouse's figure was slightly wider than the width of the carriage door. He was required to push, and as the largest part of her anatomy was the most difficult to obtain entrance to the vehicle, that, unfortunately, was the area that he had to place his hands on in order to accomplish his aim of getting his mistress inside of the coach.

"Ow!" screamed Mrs Prouse, in much discomfort, "Be careful of my operation, Pascoe. 'Tis still tender, you fool!"

The couple stood on the steps of Bosmenna, smiling and waving. Mrs Prouse, sitting in her coach surrounded by a multitude of cushions, waved farewell whilst leaning her head out of the window, calling out to them that they 'positively had to visit with her'. She would probably have said more, had the carriage not bumped over a rut in the road, which caused the poor lady to suffer much discomfort. The carriage made its way slowly down the road, accompanied by the sound of Mrs Prouse's voice haranguing her coachman unmercifully.

Archelaus turned and made his way inside, but as soon as he reached the hallway, he sat on the nearest chair and laughed until the tears ran down his face. Patience, well used to Mrs Prouse and her ways, smiled, but it gladdened her heart to see her husband give way to his mirth. It was the first time she had seen him enjoy himself so completely when in her company.

"I beg your pardon, my dear," he finally gasped once recovered from his merriment, before adding, somewhat incautiously: "No wonder her poor husband likes to drink, for I have had occasion to the do the same and can sympathise with the fellow." He took out his handkerchief to wipe the tears from his eyes and so was not aware of the crestfallen look that appeared on his wife's face at his statement.

With a swish of her skirts, she turned abruptly and headed for the parlour. Meanwhile, her husband got up from the chair, sighed and headed towards the door in order to find Thomas.

"Have you always been employed at Bosmenna, Mr Angove, sir?" enquired Archelaus conversationally, as they returned from checking the sheep in the lower meadow.

"No, Mr Hosken, sir," replied Thomas, "I used to farm with my father as a young man, but we fell upon hard times. The farm was sold and I came here to work for old Mr Polmennor. Mrs Angove was a serving girl, in the house, in those days and after a while we married and had Cissy. At about the same time, Mrs Polmennor had Patience, I mean Mrs Hosken, but her poor mother didn't live for long after the birth. Mr Polmennor was most distraught and within a few years his health began to fail. Mrs Hosken was about ten when her father died. I did of my best to help with her upbringing and managed the farm on my own for a long while. The missus became like a second mother to her but 'twas an awkward situation with Mrs Hosken, or Miss Polmennor as she was then, being our employer."

"Yes, of course," nodded the young man.

"See, 'tis hard to tell your employer what to do, Mr Hosken, sir," explained Angove, "and so she turned out a bit headstrong."

"Rather an understatement, Mr Angove," commented Archelaus, with a twitch of his lips.

"I do believe if she was shown some . . . er . . . some tenderness," advised Thomas cautiously, "then she would make a fine wife."

"Do you, Mr Angove, sir?"

"Oh, yes sir. She has a sweet and kind disposition, 'tis her stern behaviour that can be a bit difficult to deal with," he explained.

"I'm afraid I have yet to observe the 'sweet and kind disposition', Mr Angove, sir, but as regards the stern behaviour I have a considerable knowledge," Hosken advised him.

Thomas sighed, but plucking up the courage to address his employer with familiarity, suddenly said in an exasperated tone: "Have 'ee tried kissing her, sir?"

Mr Hosken went off in a peal of laughter at the thought. When he had recovered himself, he advised Mr Angove that he was not brave enough to attempt such a feat and if he were honest, he believed he would not want to do so in any case.

"But...but do 'ee feel nothing for her, sir?" asked Mr Angove, with great concern.

The young man became quiet and studied the ricks in the mowhay with great interest for a long while.

"Do you think we will have enough winter fodder, Mr Angove?" he asked, his expression inscrutable.

CHAPTER 12

PATIENCE HOSKEN turned the card over in her hand, frowning as she did so. Addressing her husband, who was sitting at the small table and slowly reading the gazette, she asked: "Have you ever heard of 'The Elixir of Lebanon', Archie?"

"No, my dear," he replied, and did not raise his head from the paper.

"Dr Abernathy says on his card that it is used to cure all manner of ailments and that it is his own concoction. He also recommends the use of his particular salve, the well-known and much admired 'Asiatic Cream of Mongolia' for afflictions of the skin and complexion. It is a preparation made from the milk of Yak mares, apparently. What are Yaks?" she asked, consumed with curiosity.

There was no reply from her husband, so she called his name; "Archie! I asked you a question! What are Yaks?"

I've no idea, my dear," he answered, but still continued to read his paper.

She stamped her foot in anger. Although she was pleased that her husband had learned his letters so well that he could attempt to read the gazette without assistance, it was very frustrating, for he took so long to even turn the page.

"Well, he says he will call again this afternoon, so I suppose I can ask him then," she decided. Watching her husband, she noticed that his lips moved with every word he read. 'Such well-shaped lips,' she thought to herself.

"Archie?"

"Yes, my dear,"

"Will you be in attendance when Dr Abernathy calls?" enquired his wife.

"That is for you to decide, my dear," he answered politely.

"I…I should very much like for you to be there, Archie," she informed him.

"Then I will attend, my dear," he confirmed.

"Thank you, Archie," she said. He lifted his head and looked at his wife and she smiled nervously at him. He regarded her calmly for a long time. Then, without changing his expression, resumed his reading of the paper.

Dr Serpentine Abernathy was most prompt in attending on the young couple that afternoon. He had called earlier that day but neither had been at home. Mr Hosken had gone to the market with his farm manager and Mrs Hosken had been riding on the cliffs with her new mare, so he had left his card and informed Mrs Angove that he would call at about two of the clock.

A tall man, of middle age and extremely well-dressed, if a little ostentatious in his attire, Dr Abernathy strode into the withdrawing room and extended his hand towards Mrs Hosken, completely ignoring her husband.

"Dear lady," he said in a booming voice, and then affected a most magnificent bow.

Archelaus raised an eyebrow, but said nothing until his wife turned to introduce him to the doctor.

"How do you do?" intoned Dr Abernathy abruptly, he then turned his attention to Mrs Hosken once more. Mr Hosken, not expecting to be shown any regard, for the circumstances of his marriage were well known, did not imagine that he was to be treated with such obvious disdain, either. Intrigued, he sat down to observe their visitor with great attention.

Tea was taken and the doctor made many references to the beneficial effects of this beverage upon the system, particularly the stomach.

Mrs Hosken agreed that she had heard much in favour of the drink, indeed, her own doctor had made the same observations.

"Ah yes," boomed Dr Abernathy, "poor Simcott." He tutted and shook his head, before announcing that it was most regrettable that the gentleman in question was of such advanced years. "If I may be so bold as to suggest that medical science has moved on at such a pace, that the poor man has been left far behind what one, such as myself, would consider good practice."

"I have always found him most knowledgeable and obliging," reprimanded Mrs Hosken in defence of her practitioner.

"Oh, my dear lady, of course. He has the most impeccable manners, but one has to move with the times, you know. A pig is most obliging in that it gives us ham, but I would not wish for such a creature to mend a broken leg, would you, ma'am?"

Mrs Hosken could do no more than agree with this, but would have said more to defend her practitioner when her husband cleared his throat and asked a question.

"Excuse my ignorance, Dr Abernathy, but what is a Yak?"

With a tight smile on his lips, the visitor turned to Mr Hosken.

"A Yak, sir, is a large bovine that lives in the upper mountains of Mongolia and other parts of the continent of Asia. The best description of it would be to say that it resembles a cow, but that it is covered with a great quantity of hair due to the cold conditions prevalent wherein it is situate."

If Dr Abernathy thought this officious statement would suffice, he was to be disappointed.

"Do they moo?" asked Archelaus, an innocent look upon his face.

"I've no idea, sir," snapped the doctor in reply.

"Are they wild creatures?" came the next question.

"Some are, but the majority are herded by the local populace," he returned abruptly.

"What are they called, the local people?" asked the young man relentlessly

"Um…" floundered the visitor, "…the Yak People!"

"They are also Yaks?" exclaimed Archelaus.

"No sir, they are merely named after their animals!" Before his questioner could ask more, he turned to Mrs Hosken and attempted to impress her with the contents of the bag he carried.

"I have here, my dear lady, a selection of the potions that I, with my own advanced medical knowledge and abilities, have endeavoured to produce in able to help my fellow man to improve the many inflictions that the human of the species has had visited upon them." With great ceremony, he then produced various labelled bottles from his bag. Immediately, the infuriating young man reached out and took hold of a small pot, unscrewed the lid, sniffed the contents, stuck his finger into it and, placing his finger in his mouth, tasted the mixture. He smacked his lips together with relish.

"That's very tasty, Dr Abernathy. You should try some, my dear," he enthused, turning to his wife briefly before asking of the doctor: "If I may be so bold, sir, what is it?"

Dr Abernathy sighed, before saying in a frustrated tone: " 'Tis my 'Asiatic salve', sir and 'tis meant to be applied to the body!"

"What part?" enquired his host.

"The part that is afflicted, sir!" retorted Dr Abernathy sharply.

"So if I have a sore tongue, I could put it on that?"

"It is not meant to be ingested, sir!" snapped the doctor, but the young man took no notice as he was busily engaged in opening another bottle. Pouring out a large amount of the liquid, he rubbed it into the back of his hand, and then flexed his fingers a few times.

"What a wonderful embrocation, Dr Abernathy! Why, my hand feels better already and it did not even feel sore before I applied this salve," rejoiced Archelaus, a beaming smile on his face.

"That is not a salve, sir! 'Tis my renowned 'Elixir of Lebanon' and it is most expensive!" He reached out and removed the bottle from the young man's hand before he could anoint himself with any more of the medication. He began to return the potions to his bag, muttering under his breath as he did so.

"Oh," cried Archie, a look of abject disappointment on his face, "don't put them away, sir, for I so like to look at all the pretty colours."

The doctor threw him a glance of angry disgust whilst Mrs Hosken regarded her husband in disbelief, but Archelaus merely beamed happily in return.

"Mrs Hosken, I am so sorry but I am most afeared that I will have to curtail my visit to your delightful abode, on the grounds that I have other patients in desperate need of my services. However, should you require my assistance at any time please do not hesitate to call upon me," he announced sharply. Bowing rather stiffly to Mrs Hosken, he informed her in a brusque tone that the visit 'had been delightful' and not bothering to say goodbye to Mr Hosken at all, he left the room, closing the door with a loud snap.

"Archie, what did you think you were doing?" demanded his wife, stunned by the actions of her husband. "Dr Abernathy must think you a fool!"

"Possibly, my dear," said Archelaus, a thoughtful expression on his face.

"To ask such stupid questions! And then you had the audacity to open those medicine bottles without even asking permission of him!" she admonished him, shocked at his conduct. "I have never known you behave in such a manner. He was most annoyed when you used so much of his 'Elixir of Lebanon', you heard him say that it was most expensive!"

"I heard and saw a lot, my dear," he told her, before continuing in a quiet voice: "but none of it led me to believe that Dr Abernathy is anything more than a charlatan!"

"Archie!"

"The 'Asiatic Cream of Mongolia' is nothing more than goose grease, scented with some rosemary, and as for his 'Elixir of Lebanon'!" and here he gave a derisory laugh, "coloured pond water, no more than that!"

"I don't believe a word of it!" cried his wife. "How would the likes of you know? Are you a man of medicine?"

"No, my dear," he answered, "but I have spent my life amongst thieves and fraudsters and I can recognise a man trying to hoodwink another in a moment!"

"But…but…" stammered his wife, shocked by this information, "he…he lanced Mrs Prouse's boil!"

Her husband's lip twitched, the twinkle appeared in his eye and before he gave way to fits of laughter, Archelaus managed to gasp: "Yes. He did, my dear, didn't he?"

CHAPTER 13

JASPER POLMENNOR sat on a rock on the beach and sniffed loudly, then wiped a tear from his cheek. Suddenly, a dog panted up to him and began to lick his face with undisguised affection.

"Hello, Rip," he said, trying to smile, but because he was full of sorrow, he was not successful.

"Hello, Jasper," called Mr Hosken as he walked across the beach towards him, following behind the dog. "What's the matter, my friend?" he asked and picking a spot beside the young man, sat down beside him.

"Father says he will get the new doctor to put me away," he explained and then began to sob brokenly.

"Now, now, Jasper," said Archelaus, putting his arm around the distraught man's shoulders consolingly, "that won't happen. I expect your father is just feeling a bit annoyed about something."

"I told him I wanted to marry Cissy and he said . . . he said that I cannot marry anyone because I'm an idiot," sobbed Jasper, "and then he said Dr Abernathy will write a letter for him and the authorities will come and put me in the asylum!" Now, the poor fellow began to cry in earnest. His companion, frowning slightly, told Jasper that he was not to worry as he was sure his father would do no such thing.

"He will, he will, Archie!" protested the sobbing youngster.

"Of course he won't, Jasper," urged Archelaus, hoping to stop the flood of tears.

"He's got him to write a letter about Patience, Archie, so he'll do one about me next," gulped Jasper, shaking in his distress.

"Dr Abernathy has written a letter about your cousin?"
Jasper nodded dumbly.

"What does the letter say, Jasper? Do you know?"

"Yes," gasped young Polmennor. He looked at his friend, the tears hanging on his eyelashes, and said: "Father gave him some money and he wrote that Cousin Patience has lost her senses and needs to go to an..." he sniffed loudly, "...an asylum! And he said…he said he will have me sent to one as well! Oh, Archie, I don't think I want to go to one because I won't get to see Cissy." He began to cry again, then turned to his friend and said sadly: "I like Cissy, Archie. She is kind to me."

Archelaus Hosken's frown deepened at Jasper's confession. He was not sure what scheme Richard Polmennor and the fraudulent doctor had decided upon, but his wife's cousin would not part with his money without good cause.

Young Mr Polmennor, sniffing and sobbing, started to speak again, "Father said he will be going to Ludgvan feast and will meet with his solicitor there. He's going to give him the letter about Patience and then they will come and take her away!"

"No they won't, Jasper," Mr Hosken assured him.

"Yes they will, Archie, and then they will come and take me away, too!" he said, and he began to howl loudly.

"They will do no such thing, Jasper, because I won't let them," stated Archelaus firmly.

Jasper stopped crying at once and stared at his friend in amazement.

"Can you do that, Archie?"

"Yes, I can, Jasper, and I will!" announced Mr Hosken in a determined voice. "Now, stop this crying and dry your eyes. Then we can walk back to the house for something to eat and you can see Cissy."

Immediately, young Polmennor's face brightened, all his worries despatched by his friend's confident assertion. Taking the handkerchief from his friend, he wiped his face and then blew his nose noisily.

"Oh, Archie!" he sighed, and smiled broadly, "I think you are the best friend I've ever had!" and he threw his arms around Archelaus and hugged him tightly.

"That will do, Jasper, that will do!" pleaded his companion, feeling the breath being squeezed out of his body by the young man's strong embrace. Jasper apologised and released Archelaus at once. They got up from the rock, and between throwing a piece of driftwood for Rip, made their way to the path at the bottom of the cliff. The Polmennor's farm and

Bosmenna both bordered the beach, so Jasper often walked down to the sea from his home. Sometimes he would meet his friend, Archie, there and they would throw sticks for Rip. Jasper liked to do that and today was of great importance for the young man because his cousin's husband had said he would not let his father put him away. All his life, young Polmennor had been told that he was going to be sent to an asylum and it had always frightened him. Now, his dear friend, Archie, was going to help him and even better than that, he was going to see Cissy again. Jasper sighed with pleasure and smiled happily at Mr Hosken.

"Ludgvan Feast? Why on earth do you want to go to that?" exclaimed an astonished Patience Hosken.

"I would like to go, my dear," replied Archelaus calmly.

Patience sighed with frustration, for her husband rarely expressed a desire to go anywhere. However, as various neighbours seemed to have accepted him into the community and the congregation at the local church now greeted them in a far friendlier manner, she felt that it would not hurt to be seen at a local feast. Why he was so fixed on going all the way to Ludgvan, however, she could not begin to understand.

"There are other feasts we could go to, Archie," she stated and fixed him with a hard stare.

"I know, my dear, but I would particularly like to go to Ludgvan," he replied quietly, yet with a degree of determination that she had never noticed in her husband before.

"Very well!" she stated in exasperation, "We will go, but for goodness sake do not embarrass me again by imbibing too much alcohol! I do not look forward to travelling back in the coach with you drunk beyond reason! Do you hear me, Archie!"

"Yes, my dear," he replied quietly.

Mr Archelaus Hosken greeted various acquaintances that they met at the feast, but refused all offers to retire to the inn for refreshment. He was accompanying his wife and did not wish to annoy her by drinking so much as one glass of alcohol in her presence. He also needed a clear head for what he was to attempt to do. Patience had allowed him some money to have about his person for once, so he had stopped at various stalls. At one he bought her some fairings, at another a bag of lavender and at the third, he purchased her some fine ribbons.

"For me, Archie?" she queried, teasingly.

"Of course, my dear," he replied, with a slight smile. His attention was now drawn to a tall man who stood alone, watching the wrestling. He was not actively engaged in following the bout between the two local farm hands, but seemed to be peering about as if he was looking for someone.

"Shall we go to greet your cousin, my dear?" enquired Archelaus.

Patience sighed loudly, and remarked: "I suppose we ought, but I would prefer not to have to speak to the man!"

"I feel the same," said her husband, "but it would be rude not to greet him."

"Yes, you are correct, Archie," she remarked and so they made their way across the field to Mr Polmennor's side.

"Hello, cousin," Mrs Hosken said.

Richard Polmennor jumped. Turning, his eyes widened in surprise to see Mr and Mrs Hosken standing before him.

"Ah…Cousin Patience, I did not expect to see you here today," he muttered in a distracted fashion.

"We decided that we ought to get about some more, did we not, Archie?"

Her husband nodded his head in agreement, but seemed more interested in going through the pockets of his jacket.

"Archie, what are you doing?" rasped his wife in an annoyed undertone, for her husband seemed to be taking out their purchases and moving them from one pocket to another.

"I did not want the fairings to taste of lavender, my dear," he explained lamely.

"Well, try and stop fidgeting, Archie!"

"Yes, my dear," he replied, observing Mr Polmennor all the while. He noticed immediately when Richard nodded his head at a small, rotund gentleman, attired very soberly, who stood by the stall of an old basket seller, who was lamely trying to attract his attention so that he would purchase some of her wares.

"I'm sorry, cousin," broke in Polmennor to Patience, somewhat excitedly, "but I have just seen an acquaintance that I have to discuss a business matter with, and I fear if I do not greet him now he will leave before I have had time to talk with him."

"Certainly, Richard," Patience replied in a bored voice, and went to turn away. However, her husband did not move and she was about to berate him, when she noticed that the lavender bag he had purchased was again in his hand. Opening her mouth to speak, it appeared that her husband had taken leave of his senses, for she thought she saw him throw the seeds of lavender all over her cousin.

"Damn this wind!" swore Archelaus, and then, full of apologies, began to brush the small seeds off her cousin's coat with a great many feverish movements of his hands. "So sorry, Mr Polmennor, I thought the bag was closed tight and when I realised that it was loose, I was attempting to retie it."

"Archie!" exclaimed his wife, shocked at his behaviour.

"I'm sorry, my dear, I should not have sworn," he apologised.

Cousin Richard, infuriated by Hosken's behaviour, pushed him away in disgust. "You might have picked less of a fool for a husband, Patience," he snapped at his cousin as he turned away. "I am of the opinion that my Jasper has more about him than this idiot!"

Mortified, Patience turned to take out her rage on her husband, but was promptly told to keep quiet.

"Don't you tell m…!" began Hosken's infuriated wife.

"Do as I tell you, wife!" Archelaus commanded in a stern voice, "and do it now!"

Before she could open her mouth to reply, her husband grabbed her arm and led her to another stall. Without asking her opinion, he purchased two bonnets, neither of which Mrs Hosken found at all fashionable. Fitting one inside the other, he swung them idly from their ribbons.

"Archie, I…" she began, her eyes darting fire at him.

"Wife!" snapped her husband, "Keep that pretty mouth shut, speak when you are spoken to and deny everything!"

Just at that moment, a cry of rage could be heard and within a very short space of time, Richard Polmennor came running towards them, with the rotund stranger and James Trenear following him as quickly as they could.

"You damn thief, Hosken! You have stolen my property. Search him, Trenear and you will find about his person a sealed document addressed to Mr. Williams here!" he panted, out of breath with exertion.

"I beg your pardon, Cousin Richard?" exclaimed Archelaus.

"Don't you 'Cousin Richard' me, you damnable pickpocket!" shouted Polmennor. By this time, a small crowd had surrounded the group to observe the spectacle.

James Trenear told Mr Hosken to empty his pockets.

"I will not!" Archelaus told him stoutly, but Mr Trenear, far more in the clutches of Mr Polmennor than he would ever care to admit, seized his person and began searching through Mr Hosken's pockets himself. He threw the ribbons and the fairings to the floor, the few remaining coins he found followed, but in the end he turned to his friend and shook his head in exasperation.

"Nothing, Mr Polmennor," he intoned in his deep voice.

"Of course he has it somewhere!" shouted Polmennor, and then he noted that Patience stood by her husband's side with her mouth firmly shut. "She has it!" he cried, "Empty your reticule, Patience, for you are in league with this damn scoundrel!"

Patience clasped her reticule firmly in her hand but Richard wrenched it away from her, upended it and shook the contents into the mud. A small purse of money, a hair comb and a handkerchief was all it contained. He threw the reticule to the floor and stamped on it in temper.

Turning to Archelaus, he caught hold of his necktie and pulled him towards him glaring at him with a furious expression on his face.

"If I ever discover that you have that document, you filthy vagabond, I'll break your damn neck, do you understand?"

Archelaus coughed. "Perfectly!" he wheezed in reply and was promptly released and pushed to one side. Polmennor turned on his heel and without saying another word, marched away.

Archelaus shook his head, straightened his necktie and then bent down and retrieved his wife's belongings, before picking up his own.

"I'm sorry, my dear," he said calmly, "but your ribbons and fairings are covered in mud. Shall I purchase you some more?"

"No, Archie, you will not!" snapped his wife, simmering with rage, "I have never, never been so embarrassed in my life! We are going home, at once! Is that understood?"

"Yes, my dear," replied Archie wearily, and trudged after her with his head down, swinging the bonnets by their ribbons as he walked.

CHAPTER 14

IN THE dining room at Bosmenna, Mrs Hosken turned to Archelaus and opened her mouth, intent on berating her husband yet again for his behaviour. She had not given him a minute's peace all the way from Ludgvan, but he had not made a single reply during the entire journey.

Hosken turned away before his wife had a chance to speak, went to the door and called for Mrs Angove to fetch her husband.

"Please to send him here immediately, Mrs Angove, for I have great need of his assistance," he told her authoritatively.

Betty Angove blinked in surprise, for she had never been addressed by Mr Hosken in such a manner before, but she did as she was told and within a short space of time, her husband was standing in the dining room with the couple.

Mrs Hosken was completely at a loss to see the change that had come over her husband. She tried again to tell him off, but he merely told her, most politely, to hold her tongue.

Picking up the bonnets from the table, he separated them and a sealed letter fell out and landed on the table.

"Archie!" cried his shocked wife, "You did steal Richard's letter, after all. How could you!"

"Mr Angove, would you be so kind as to read this for me, sir," enquired Archelaus quietly.

"I can't break the seal, sir!" exclaimed Thomas aghast.

"Then I will have to do it," sighed Archelaus.

With the seal broken, Mr Angove was again instructed to read the contents by Mr Hosken.

Slowly, Angove divulged that Dr Serpentine Abernathy had made a detailed examination of Mrs Patience Hosken and had concluded without doubt that in his revered medical opinion, she was suffering from severe delusions. For her own safety, she should be placed in a correctional institution until such time as she could return to her senses. Dr Abernathy then listed a great number of medical establishments of which he had been a principal or director and even mentioned two that he had founded personally.

Shocked, Patience slumped into a chair. Thoughtfully, Archie again called for Mrs Angove and requested her to bring them some tea.

"But...but..." stammered Mrs Hosken, "he never examined me at all! And the whole time he was with us, it was you that played the fool, Archie!"

Mr Angove, frowning, turned to Archelaus and asked him to explain the events that led up to his theft of the letter.

Briefly, Hosken told him of the conversation that he had held with Jasper, he also informed him that it was his belief, that Dr Abernathy was not a doctor at all and that he was attempting to perpetrate a fraud within the community. Richard Polmennor was determined to get his hands on Bosmenna, using fair means or foul, and sought to use the fellow to achieve his ends.

Thomas nodded his head and then scratched his chin, wondering how best to proceed.

"If we go to your lawyer, Mrs Hosken, we have to admit Archie's guilt, for there were a fair many witnesses at the feast, I should imagine, who would have seen the affray," he told her.

Sadly, Mrs Hosken nodded, but said nothing as she was still bemused by what had happened.

"I imagine that, should Polmennor's lawyer succeed in having Mrs Hosken sent away, then it would not be long before Mr Trenear could be encouraged to lay some trifling theft upon myself and I would find myself incarcerated, or worse," mused Archelaus, to which comment Thomas nodded sombrely in agreement. They talked for a long while, attempting to find a solution to the problem. Of course, it was no guarantee that the action Polmennor was attempting to take against his cousin would succeed, but Williams was a clever lawyer and Patience had not been considered to be the wisest woman in West Penwith by taking a common thief for a husband. Hardly the action of a woman with a sound mind, pointed out her husband with a sigh. Silence fell upon the room until a gleam came into Mr Hosken's eye. He turned to his friend with a hopeful look upon his face.

"I do not like to suggest this, Mr Angove, sir, but I have noted that you are an immensely strong man. At the top of this letter, Dr, or should I say, Mr Abernathy has conveniently put his address. Would it be in order for us to make a visit to his humble abode and…er…entice him to alter this document, or even to destroy it altogether?" he asked innocently.

Thomas grinned and said: "I'll get me flintlock," and turned and left the room immediately.

"Oh Archie, Archie! What you must think of me for disbelieving you. What can I say?" said his wife, her voice full of contrition.

"Well, to be honest, my dear, my head is still ringing from all you said to me on the way back from the feast, so I would appreciate your silence for once," replied her husband promptly. Calling to Rip, he left the room and headed off to arrange for the carriage to be brought out once more.

At midnight, Mr Angove, Mr Hosken and Rip returned to Bosmenna; they made a rather noisy entrance but Patience, Betty and Cissy were awake and seated in the dining room. It was obvious Mrs Polmennor had been crying, for there were tearstains on her cheeks.

Mr Angove, smiling broadly, walked across to where she was sitting and placed two letters in front of her. The first intimated that Serpentinc Abernathy, otherwise known as Clem Gripe, formerly a footman from a hotel in Bath, was not and never had been a member of the medical fraternity. The second was full of contrite and abject apologies to Mrs Hosken and her family for any distress that had been caused to her, his devout wish being that she would not be taking any further proceedings over the small misunderstanding that had occurred between them.

"He'll still be able to carry on making fools of people though," sobbed Patience.

"Not in Cornwall, my dear," Archelaus encouraged her with a smile, "He was persuaded to leave this fair county. In fact, I think if he could swim from St Ives this very night, he would attempt to do so!"

"Probably more comfortable than him having to sit in the mail coach, I should think, Mr Hosken, sir, after the way Rip went for 'en when 'ee went to run out the back door," grinned Thomas.

"Rip seems to have a fondness for biting that particular part of the anatomy, don't you, boy?" At which point the dog barked and wagged his tail in agreement.

"We threw the so-called medicines - and his bag - into the harbour and told him that if he was not out of the county by this time tomorrow, then we would be calling on him again," Archelaus said, "and this time we would make no attempt to call off our dog." He pursed his lips and added: "He assured us, on his knees, that he would never visit this county again and, I must admit, I do believe him, for he shook most dramatically, did he not, Mr Angove?"

"Most dramatically, sir," laughed Thomas, then catching sight of the intense expression on Patience Hosken's face, coughed and suggested that he thought it late enough that they should think of retiring for the night.

After the Angoves had left the couple alone, Patience attempted, falteringly, to tell her husband of her gratitude for all he had done on her behalf.

"I would say more, Archie, but as Thomas said it is late and I think we should retire ourselves, don't you agree?"

"Yes, my dear," replied her husband, but continued to read the letters that they had obtained from the fraudulent practitioner, smiling as he did so.

"I am sure that I will never be able to express my thanks to you adequately, Archie," Patience told him, attempting to get some response from her spouse.

"No matter, my dear," he answered, abstractedly.

"I'll go up now, shall I, Archie?"

"If you wish, my dear," replied her husband, still absorbed in his reading.

"I'll…I'll wish you goodnight, Archie," she said in a dulcet tone.

"Goodnight, my dear," replied Archelaus, turning his attention to the second of the two letters.

He heard the swish of her dress as she turned from him, followed by a loud bang as she slammed the door.

Raising his eyebrows, he shrugged his shoulders and slowly finished the letter, before picking up the solitary candle, calling to Rip and then retiring to his room.

CHAPTER 15

THAT morning, Betty Angove dropped the mail in front of Mrs Hosken as she always did, but today, instead of turning around and leaving the room, in her normal manner, she walked all the way to the chair by the window and held out a single letter to Mr Hosken.

Archelaus stared at her bemusedly, for he was never the recipient of any item that came through the post. Any invitations that were addressed to both of them, were invariably opened by his wife. However, this letter was different because it did not contain a reference to Mrs Hosken in the address; it was his name alone that appeared on the direction.

"Thank…thank you, Mrs Angove," he stammered in surprise. Getting up from his seat, he made his way to where his wife sat at the round table by the window, clutching the letter in his hand.

Frowning, she watched his approach and when he arrived at the table, motioned him to a chair by her side.

"I…I have a letter, my dear," he said awkwardly.

"So I see, Archie. Are you wishful to open it?"

"I've never had a letter before," he explained nervously, "what do you think it is about?"

"Well," proclaimed Patience, determinedly, "you won't know that until you have opened it, Archie!"

With shaking hands, he broke open the seal and attempted to read it. Although he could read fairly well, it always took him a considerable time and when he came across a long word, or one that he did not understand, he would find Thomas and ask him the meaning. However this particular morning, Mr Angove was at the next farm helping with a difficult foaling and was not at Bosmenna. Archelaus could wait until he returned, but that might be a considerable time later in the day. He had seen at a glance that the letter contained a large number of words that he did not recognise and he raised his eyes to his wife, blushing with embarrassment. Patience returned his gaze steadily. She was not feeling in the best of moods with her husband, for no matter how hard she tried to be obliging to him, he would still forsake her at the first opportunity to go out about the farm with Thomas or, if occasion demanded it, further afield. She had assumed that, by displaying a more conciliatory tone to her husband he would realise that her sentiments towards him had undergone a considerable change. However, the infuriating man seemed not to notice and so she continued to spend the greater part of each day bereft of his company.

"Would you like me to read it for you, Archie?" she asked in a matter-of-fact tone.

He nodded and passed over the paper to her. As she began to recite the contents, however, her voice trailed away to silence as she took note of that which she read.

"It's my letter!" said Archelaus, sulkily, aggrieved that Patience was reading the letter to herself and not to him at all.

"I'm sorry, Archie, forgive me. I was just so amazed at the contents," she explained, and placing it on the table, read out every word to her husband. The letter has been sent by a lawyer, by the name of Marsh, who had been given the responsibility of discharging the estate of the late Mr Archelaus Prendergast Hosken, of Valparaiso, South America, but formerly of Colchester, England. The last will and testament of the aforementioned gentleman detailed that all his assets were left to his only son, known as Archelaus Hosken, and believed to have been placed with a travelling family when still a small child, due to the ill health of the infant's mother.

Mr Marsh went on to explain in great detail that he had spent almost a year searching for a Mr Hosken that would appear to be the son of the deceased. Upon receiving information concerning a certain Archelaus Hosken of Bosmenna, he deduced that this was the gentleman that he had spent so much time seeking. He would be calling at the house that afternoon, with further information that he would need to impart to the young man known to reside at Bosmenna with that name, and to ascertain that the gentleman in question was indeed the correct inheritor of the estate.

Archie raised a worried face to his smiling wife. "This is good news for you, Archie, for, if you are indeed the person Mr

Marsh is seeking, then not only will you hear details of your family that were hitherto unknown to you, but you are to receive an inheritance as well!" she announced reassuringly.

Dazed, he looked down at the letter again and said softly: "But if I am not, then I would appear to be as worthless as I was before." Picking up the letter, he folded it, placed it in his pocket and got up to leave the room.

"Archie, I do not think that of you now, and I can assure you that your letter makes no difference," said his wife, placing her hand upon his arm. She wanted to say more, but her husband bowed stiffly and turned away from her, heading for the door.

"Archie, you do believe me, don't you?" she queried, desolated by his reaction to her statement.

"Of course, my dear," he replied mechanically, and left the room.

That afternoon, Mr Percival Marsh was shown into the withdrawing room of Bosmenna and was confronted by the young man he had travelled so far to find. As Mr Hosken's mother's family was known to him, he was much struck by the resemblance that the gentleman had to certain members of that household. However, it would require more than looks alone to ascertain that this person should receive his presumed father's legacy. He noted that, uncommonly, it was the spouse - Mrs Hosken - who made the introductions and seemed to take charge of the proceedings, indeed, her husband appeared to be struck dumb by the entire meeting.

However, as Mr Marsh began to explain that he would need proof to verify that the Archelaus Hosken he was seeking was indeed the person who was sitting opposite to him, the gentleman put his hand in his pocket and withdrew a small bonnet and a solitary earring, placing them on the table.

The lawyer beamed delightedly and producing a small leather case, removed from it another earring, a perfect match for the one lying on the table, and carefully placed the two together.

He held out his hand again to the young man and said delightedly: "How do you do, Mr Archelaus Hosken. You do not know what pleasure it gives me to greet you after so long attempting to find you."

"I expect you will want to know about some details of your past that I am able to furnish you with. Can you remember anything at all of your family?" he asked kindly.

"Nothing, sir," replied Archelaus, shaking his head sadly.

"Never fear, sir, I think I can most definitely help you there," replied Mr Marsh with an understanding smile.

"Your mother, Miss Constance Gascoigne, a member of the Gascoigne family of Fillerton Manor, became enamoured of a young gentleman of the name of Archelaus Prendergast Hosken, an itinerant carpenter, recently released from the navy after having been press ganged from Polperro as a very young man. Miss Gascoigne's family forbade them to meet but the couple, being young and very much in love, ignored these strictures. Upon reaching the age of twenty-one, Miss Constance asked permission to marry your father. This permission was not granted, so she packed a bag and left her home forever. Obviously, she was a young woman with a very determined disposition." Archie glanced surreptitiously at his wife at this remark, but she was staring with great interest as Mr Marsh spoke

"They married and your father found employment. Within a year, their marriage was blessed with a happy event, namely your birth, Mr Hosken, and you were duly christened in the local church. I have a copy of the parish register here for you to see," and he produced a piece of paper, which he handed to Archelaus, who stared at it bemusedly. "For the first year of your existence everything seemed to prosper. But, unfortunately, Mr Hosken senior lost his employment and had to seek work further afield."

Archelaus, listening to a history that he thought never to hear, found it difficult to follow the events that the lawyer was detailing to him. His brow creased as he tried hard to concentrate on that being recounted to him. His father, having no success in getting a position locally, joined a ship sailing for South America, where miners and other itinerants were required by a large mining concern. He left all his possessions in the care of his wife, assuring her that when he had enough money, she and their young son would be sent for to begin their new life in another country. Shortly after he left, his wife became ill. Piece by piece, she sold her jewels and then sold all those items that had belonged to his father to pay for the medicines required. She wrote to her family and asked for assistance, but her father replied that he wished for no communication from her, for he would not assist her in the life she had chosen. Realising the perilous state of health that she was in and not wishing for her son to be abandoned to the evils of the local orphanage, she arranged for him to be taken care of by a travelling family that she had come to know. A woman from this particular community had been most concerned when Mr Hosken's mother had been taken ill in the local market.

"Granny Jacobs," whispered Archelaus. "She was called Granny Jacobs and she had the kindest of hearts." Patience stared in surprise at her husband, for he had never mentioned the name of any member of his previous acquaintances before. "After Granny Jacobs died, I lived with different families and as I got older, I moved between different groups of travellers. Because I knew no other, Mr Marsh, I have to admit that I enjoyed the life. All you are telling me seems almost to refer to another person."

Mr Marsh smiled sympathetically at the young man, who appeared most despondent. He cleared his throat and continued with his narrative, explaining with great gentleness that Mr Hosken's mother had died soon after Archelaus had been placed with the travellers. Mr Hosken senior did not know of what had happened until he wrote home for his family to join him in his new life. Your mother's family had claimed her remains, as they wished for them to be interred in the family crypt."

Archelaus snorted in disgust, and enquired angrily; "Was she worth more to them in death than in life, sir?"

"I'm afraid that is how it appears, sir," he replied gently, "But to resume my story, the letter was forwarded on to the Gascoignes, because that was the family that the authorities knew about. If the Gascoignes had not claimed her for their family, sir, I would not be sitting here with you today for it would not have been possible to trace you. When she died, your mother had left certain documents, along with the matching earring, in which she had written an account of what had happened to you so that her husband would be able to trace you if, and when, he returned. The Gascoignes sent all that she had left to your father when they informed him what had happened to his wife. I can supply very little information to you concerning your father other than to tell you that for many years he worked in and around various mines in South America. He sent money home to the Gascoignes for your upkeep should they ever find you. However, your mother's family made no attempt to look for you and merely directed the small amounts they received into a fund in your name, which was administered by my father's firm of solicitors. Time passed and eventually, your father received some good fortune when he sold a piece of land that he had purchased on which had been discovered a rich vein of silver. He sent home by packet ship all his possessions, including the money that had accrued to him through his investments and arranged to follow on a few weeks later. Unfortunately, sir, he passed away before he was able to begin his journey, his health having been affected by the adverse conditions he had experienced during his life working in some very inhospitable places on that continent."

"Those possessions came to our firm, sir, because they were intended for you. Your mother's family became aware of this fact and when they discovered that your father had sent home a considerable sum of money, they tried to claim it for their own family. My father, disgusted by their attitude, determined that you would be found and I was instructed to carry out the work. You see, if I could not find you, then the money would pass back through your mother to her family, as your father had no relatives."

Archelaus nodded, but his face registered his complete and utter bewilderment. He had awoken that morning as nothing more than a former traveller, married to a local landowner, whose position in society bordered on a tolerated interloper. Now, he was being told that he was a person of some substance, but the suddenness of this discovery left him struggling to understand this strange development.

"Perhaps I should let you have sight of this document, sir, for it is a draft on my father's bank for a large part of the money that has accrued to you. The rest will be deposited in your bank when all the details have been agreed," he said with a smile, passing over another sheet of paper into the shaking hands of Mr Hosken.

Archelaus stared at the amount written down on the paper and swallowed. He had never seen such a large figure in his life before.

"Ten thousand pounds!" he gasped, "Is that what this says, sir?" and he shook his head in disbelief.

"No, sir, I'm afraid you have that incorrectly," Mr Marsh said quietly, but before he could continue, the young man, blushing furiously explained that his education had started late in life, adding that a thousand would be a very agreeable figure, for it was far more than he had ever expected to receive.

"I'm sure it would, sir, but the amount written here is not one thousand but one hundred thousand pounds," the amused lawyer informed him.

Archelaus opened his mouth, but no words came. Turning to his wife and with a shaking finger, he pointed to the figure on the draft. He tried to speak but the shock that he had received overcame him. He managed only to utter "Good God" before he fell from his chair in a deep faint.

CHAPTER 16

A WEEK had passed since the visit from Mr Marsh and, naturally, in that time much had changed for Mr Hosken. With the advice of his wife, herself still reeling with disbelief at what had happened, Archelaus had opened a bank account for the first time in his life. A local solicitor had been appointed to act for him on any business matters that he wished to undertake and Mr Marsh continued to represent him concerning his late father's estate.

A continuous stream of visitors found it incumbent upon them to call upon the Hoskens and Archelaus discovered that he preferred the company of Mr Angove more than ever before. It was preferable to be from the house when his neighbours and new friends called, so it was inevitable that his wife seemed as far apart as before. Patience Hosken found that she had her own position to consider. Previously she had, through threats, managed to control and intimidate her husband. With the sudden advancement of his financial position, she could no longer use any of her previous methods to bring her spouse to heel. For a woman with such a controlling temperament, it was a novel experience. It was also plain to her that Archelaus Hosken had not changed his attitude to her in the slightest degree. The meals were conducted with the same icy formality as before and, Patience realised, to make any overtures of friendship towards her husband would be to rank her amongst the host of new-found friends that called with such annoying regularity.

With Christmas fast approaching, Mr Hosken asked his wife if it would be in order for him to hold a party in celebration of the festivities for the workforce.

"Archie, you do not need to ask my permission," she informed him, in a matter of fact way.

"Oh, I'm sorry. I did not realise, my dear," he replied, then became most thoughtful.

"Could I buy a farm with my money?" he asked suddenly.

His wife, surprised, stared at him, then informed him that with the funds he had available, he could buy a considerable number of farms if he so wished.

He blinked in astonishment. Although aware that he had received a large fortune, it was still a sum of money which, because of its vastness, held no meaning for him. He did not wish to visit the local towns, or even seemed disinclined to spend any of his income, not because he was miserly, but more because he had never been in such a position in his life and could not comprehend that he could buy anything that took his fancy if he so desired.

"I think I should like to buy a farm then, my dear," he told her, "and Mr Angove would be the best person to advise me."

"Yes, Thomas would be able to guide you, certainly if you had it in mind to buy locally, for he knows the area better than any man around," she told him briskly, though she was troubled that her husband should be thinking of setting up home away from Bosmenna.

"Well," announced Archelaus with new found decisiveness, "that is what I shall do, my dear."

When Mr Hosken asked Thomas to help him, Mr Angove felt a great disloyalty to his mistress in undertaking such a commission, but Mr Hosken being his employer, he had no choice in the matter.

As luck would have it, the farm next to Richard Polmennor's property was in the process of being sold, but the owner, a widow, had not accepted any of the offers that had been made to her. Thomas knew it well, but was most surprised when the young man did not request to see it and merely asked him if he could make the arrangements to buy it on his behalf.

"I trust you to know its worth, Mr Angove," he informed him, "and as I have no knowledge whatsoever as to how to go about the business, I would be most pleased if you would see to the matter for me."

"Of course, Mr Hosken, but I shall be some sad to see 'ee go from 'ere," he told him sincerely.

Archelaus Hosken did not look too happy himself and merely smiled sadly at him.

Of course, when the purchase price had been agreed, Mr Angove and Archelaus needed to go to Penzance to visit with the solicitor to sign the various documents. Mr Hosken made his signature and Thomas rose to go, but Archelaus, displaying surprising confidence, asked him to wait outside as he had further business of a private nature that he wished to conduct with his solicitor.

"Of course, Mr Hosken, sir," replied Mr Angove to his employer, though his heart ached; in all probability, the possibility of an official separation between Archie and Patience was the only private matter that Mr Hosken would need to discuss with his solicitor.

On the way back from Penzance, neither man had much to say. Mr Hosken, now a landowner in his own right, did not seem overly impressed with this fact and Thomas was sick to his soul that the young couple had not found a way through their difficulties to make their marriage work. They passed Richard and Jasper Polmennor on their way, but Angove and Hosken, sitting in the carriage, merely waved an acknowledgement. Richard Polmennor threw Archelaus an angry look, whilst Jasper smiled his normal happy grin.

"He's a sweet lad," observed Archelaus, referring to Polmennor's son.

"He is that, Mr Hosken," agreed Thomas, "and for all his lack of education and ability he had much about him to admire. 'Tis a shame that Mr Polmennor can only see what it is that the boy lacks about him and not what there is to appreciate."

In response to an enquiring look from Hosken, Angove explained that, although Jasper had little understanding on some matters, on others, such as animal husbandry, he was remarkably astute.

"Don't ask me how he does it, Mr Hosken, sir, but Jasper Polmennor can pick out the best animal from its fellows as if by instinct. And he has other qualities as well. Have 'ee ever seen the boy plough?"

Archelaus shook his head.

"Straight as a die!" confirmed Thomas, and there was no doubting the admiration he felt for the lad.

"Cissy likes him," observed Mr Hosken. Angove nodded his head and smiled bitterly, before saying: "She can like him forever, Mr Hosken, sir, for Richard Polmennor will not have his son to wed with my maid and that's a fact!"

On this astute observation, the carriage arrived in front of the house and Mr Hosken got out, clutching his papers in his hand. He turned to Thomas and informed him that he would see him after he had lunched and ran up the steps before disappearing into the house.

When his wife asked him if the farm had been purchased, Archelaus Hosken nodded his head and told her that it had. However, he made no other statement concerning the property so Patience asked: "And what do you intend to do with your farm, Archie?"

He thought for a moment, helped himself to another piece of pigeon pie and then said, simply, "Nothing, my dear."

"Nothing!" she exclaimed, taken aback with his lack of interest in the first acquisition of property that he had ever made.

He nodded, but concentrated on eating his food and had nothing further to add. His wife gave him a withering look, but realised that her husband was, as usual, not in a mood for conversation and so the meal continued in silence.

The following morning, Richard Polmennor galloped into Bosmenna, jumped from his horse and, without waiting to hand the animal over to a stable boy, ran up the steps to the house. It was most apparent that he was in an extremely bad mood. He rapped on the door and upon gaining admittance, encountered Cissy Angove and demanded the master of the house.

"Mr Hosken is about the farm, sir, but Mrs Hosken is in the withdrawing room if you would like me..." but she got no further, for after throwing his hat and gloves at her, Mr Polmennor strode away and with the briefest of knocks, entered the room where Patience sat.

Patience looked up in surprise, for the cousins had exchanged only the briefest of nods whenever they had met since the tumultuous events at Ludgvan Feast.

"Richard!" exclaimed Mrs Hosken, taken aback by his sudden entrance. Polmennor, with a thunderous look upon his face, was not intending to waste time on pleasantries with her.

"Do you know what that damn man has done?"

"Do you mean Archie, cousin?" enquired Patience.

"Of course, I do! Why, that blasted man has bought the farm next to mine, under my nose. I have been in negotiation with the Widow Semmons for more than a six-month and now she tells me that she has sold to your husband!" he ranted, breathing heavily.

"Mrs Semmons could sell to whom she wished," returned Patience, "and if Archie wanted to buy it, there was nothing to stop him. I presume that Mrs Semmons did not believe that you were to make a higher offer," she stated.

"Make a higher offer!" her cousin almost screamed, "I was attempting to get it for less than she wanted! And I would have succeeded were it not for that interfering oaf that you have married!"

"He is not an oaf!" declared Patience, springing to her husband's defence, "and if he wishes to spend his money acquiring farms, it is no concern of yours!"

"That fool of a husband of yours would not have the wit to do what he has done, Patience! 'Tis you! You have set him on to do this, and no doubt that the next farm bordering my property that comes up for sale will be taken into your net as well! You damned underhand scoundrel!" he shouted.

Knowing that she could not make any reference to Richard's own underhand practice concerning Dr Abernathy, for fear of implicating her husband, Mrs Hosken could only reiterate that she had not influenced her husband to buy the farm.

"He wanted to buy a farm using some of his inheritance, Cousin Richard! It is no business of mine how he wishes to spend his money!" she fumed, her dark eyes blazing with temper.

Richard Polmennor strode across the room and seizing her arm, he pulled her to her feet. With his face inches from her own, he continued to shout at her.

"No business of yours!" he scoffed, "Why, you damned witch, you have sought to bring me down at every turn and have used that damn wastrel to do it! Well, what good did it do you, fair Patience? He has no need of you now! Rich as Croesus, so word has it, and 'twill not be long before he throws you over for another, more accommodating baggage. You might have won this battle, Cousin, but you will lose him to another 'ere long, you mark my words! I'll admit I've lost but I shall wait to see you humbled by him with great pleasure. Such clever scheming, to think you could do me down, only to find yourself with just Bosmenna for company! Did you think no one talked of the goings on here? You fool!" He laughed, suddenly and harshly. "Why, I could almost feel sorry for the fellow: to have been forced to marry you, only to discover that he has no need for your roof over his head! How he must rue the day he said 'I will' at the church!"

He shook her roughly and then asked maliciously, "Is it warm in your empty bed, dear Cousin?"

Colour flooded into Patience's face and tears sprang to her eyes, but Richard Polmennor only laughed the more at her discomfort. However, they both turned in consternation when there came an angry voice from the doorway:

"Unhand my wife, sir!"

CHAPTER 17

SOMETHING about the way the threat was uttered made Polmennor leave hold of his cousin immediately. Now it was his turn to look embarrassed and he turned from Patience to face her irate husband. In spite of all he had said to his cousin, Richard Polmennor recognised the look of an angry spouse when he saw it.

"I...I did not hear you come in...um...Cousin Archie," he stammered awkwardly.

Archelaus Hosken strode into the room, his brow furrowed and with an angry glint in his eye. Turning to his wife, he asked with concern: "Are you alright, my dear?" She nodded, and dashing a tear from her eye resumed her seat. Her heart was pounding, though not because of the treatment she had just received from her cousin.

"I presume you have called to discuss the matter of the purchase I have just made?" enquired Archie abruptly.

"Well...well yes, Hosken, I have and...and, well damn it, man, I'm not best pleased!" Polmennor admitted disgustedly.

"And I am not best pleased that you should arrive at Bosmenna and behave in such a fashion to my wife!" snapped Archelaus in return.

"Ah...quite...heat of the moment...I...I..." blustered Richard.

"Apologise, sir, for the distress you have caused today and that which you have attempted to cause in the past towards your cousin!"

"So it was y..." but realising that he was not in a position to admit to anything either, Cousin Richard swallowed his pride and turned to his cousin, offering his abject apologies. She inclined her head to accept and to hide the smile that was attempting to break out on her lips as she witnessed Richard Polmennor's obvious discomfort.

Archelaus watched the proceeding with his own smile curling his lips. He then retraced his steps to the door and called for Mrs Angove to bring some tea and to send her husband to them also.

Thomas arrived a few moments later with his wife and Patience assumed that her husband, not the tallest of men, would find it helpful to have Angove's physical strength to support him in any further confrontations with her cousin. Although she thought Archie was giving the appearance of a man completely in control of the proceedings and would have no need for Thomas to be present.

Mrs Angove poured the tea, her face expressionless, but when she turned to leave, Mr Hosken asked her to stay.

"I think I have something to say which you may wish to hear, Mrs Angove," he told her. Taking a key from his pocket, he walked to the small desk by the window, unlocked one of the drawers and returned with the papers he had obtained from the solicitor when he made his purchase of the disputed farm.

Richard Polmennor leaned forward in his chair, breathing heavily, his anger at the events of the morning had left him in a state of unresolved tension.

"As you know, I have purchased Porthmenna farm, previously owned by Mrs Semmons," stated Archelaus quietly, but here Richard Polmennor interrupted him and asked angrily:

"Well, now that you own it, what will you be doing with the damn place? Fencing me about by buying more land, I shouldn't wonder!" he snapped.

"I purchased it, Mr Polmennor but I do not own it," Archelaus announced in his quiet way. This statement shocked the assembled company into silence. Turning to Mr Angove, Archelaus placed the papers into his hand.

"Would you read this for me Mr Angove, sir," he asked.

Thomas, looking dumbfounded at his employer, spread open the documents and began to read but when he saw the name of the new owner of Porthmenna, the words dried on his tongue. His hand began to shake and he turned to Mr Hosken in disbelief.

" 'Tis…'tis my name, Archie," he gasped, his mouth hanging open in surprise.

"Yes, Thomas," stated Archelaus simply, "I have made a gift to the man who, in my opinion, made a man of me. I hope, most sincerely, that it will please you to accept it." He heard Mrs

Angove begin to sob and turned to see her wiping the tears from her cheeks with her apron.

"But…but…" stammered Angove, as Archelaus moved towards him with his hand extended.

"I said a gift, but in reality I should have called it a payment. Please to accept it, Thomas, for…" and he turned towards his wife, who smiled at him reassuringly, "…for Patience and I would like that."

Tears hanging on his lashes, Thomas, unable to speak, caught hold of the extended hand and pulled Archelaus to him, crushing him in a bear hug of gratitude.

"Thank you, Thomas," gasped Archelaus, almost suffocated by having his head buried in the man's chest, "but I think that will do."

Angove released him and, still shaking his head in wonder, held out his arms to his wife, who rushed forward to be enfolded into his comforting embrace.

Richard Polmennor, still frowning, growled at him: "But why, man? Why did you do that?"

"I appreciate the worth of others, Mr Polmennor. 'Tis a shame that you do not," he informed him.

Polmennor blushed, "If you had a son the likes of Jasper, you would find it hard, Hosken!" he informed him bitterly.

"Possibly, Mr Polmennor, but then I think your son has much in him to be admired," Archelaus said softly.

"Do you? Damned if I can see it!" snorted Richard.

"He seems to have set his heart on a very suitable young woman, don't you think?" prompted Mr Hosken.

"Cissy? You think that Cissy Angove…" but his voice trailed off and a gleam began to form in his eye.

"Well," suggested Hosken, grinning, "the only child of a respected local landowner would seem an appropriate choice to make for a wife for Jasper, do you not agree?" Polmennor, realising that the predicament of his son looked set to be solved with far more ease than he had ever before considered possible, returned Hosken's smile.

"Forgive me again, Cousin Patience, for disturbing you, but I've got to make my way home at once," said Richard, in a tone of voice that she had never previously heard. Standing up, he offered his hand to his cousin, then shook Archelaus by the hand with unbridled enthusiasm. He even went so far as to slap him on the back and told him with a warm grin that: "He was a damn fine fellow!" Clasping Thomas Angove about the shoulders, he began to lead him from the room, advising him that the lower meadow at Porthmenna was subject to flooding, and it would make sense if they formulated some action between them to channel the water more appropriately. Their voices could be heard from the hallway as Mr Polmennor made his way to the door.

Mrs Angove, her arms outstretched, hugged and kissed Mrs Hosken and then turned to Mr Hosken, and said shyly: "Oh sir, what a treasure my sweet Patience found in 'ee," and proceeded to hug him as well. Betty Angove was short of stature but strong of arm and Archelaus emerged from her embrace rather pink in the face.

"Thank you, Mrs Angove," he uttered, struggling to regain his breath, then added, with some concern: "Will it be long before lunch is to be served?"

"You'm a little devil, Mr Hosken," giggled Mrs Angove with unusual familiarity, then turned to leave.

When the couple were alone, Patience looked shyly at her husband and smiled before stating: "That was an extremely kind and generous action on your part, Archie."

"Was it, my dear?"

"I'm very proud of you, Archie," she told him lovingly.

"Um…thank you, my dear," he muttered awkwardly, and informing her abruptly that he had need of words with Thomas, he left the room hurriedly. Patience sighed, marvelling that her husband could resolve other people's happiness, but not their own.

At lunch, his wife continued to smile at him with great affection, but Archelaus, absorbed in eating his food, seemed not to notice. They were just finishing their meal when Jasper Polmennor arrived and stuck his head around the dining room door.

"Can I come in, Archie?" he beamed.

Archelaus nodded and Jasper tumbled into the room, almost falling over his feet with excitement.

"I'm to marry Cissy, Archie!" he exclaimed with delight, "Father says I can and Mother is delighted too and she says Cissy must come for tea on Sunday and she says you and Patience must come too for tea soon and…" but Archie held up his hand to stop the flow.

"That will do, Jasper," he said with a smile and then enquired if Jasper had asked Cissy to marry him in all the excitement.

A worried look crossed the young man's face immediately. "No, Archie, I haven't," he said in trepidation.

"Well go and ask her then," laughed Archelaus.

"I will, I will!" announced an excited Jasper, who left the room at a run.

Within two minutes he was back to inform them that Cissy had said yes. He clapped his hands together with glee and beamed at his friend. Archelaus wiped his lips with his napkin and stood up, smiling at Jasper's delight.

"And have you kissed Cissy yet?" he asked, a twinkle in his eye.

Dumbfounded, Jasper shook his head and was directed to go and kiss his fiancée at once.

"It's great fun, Jasper, you'll like it," Archelaus assured him.

Jasper needed no second telling and, with a huge grin upon his face, disappeared again.

Patience got up from her chair and moved to stand in front of her husband.

"Is kissing great fun, Archie?" she asked coyly.

"Um…Yes, it is," responded her husband, taken aback by her approach.

"Do you think we ought to try it?" she enquired, her eyes dancing.

"Well…um…I…" stammered her husband.

"Is this what you do, Archie?" she asked provocatively, pouting her lips as she lifted up her face towards him.

He gulped. "Yes," he replied, in scarcely more than a whisper.

"I'm waiting, Archie," she informed him.

"Yes, my dear, but I thought you…" he began to explain.

"Well you thought wrongly, my darling," she admonished him gently, "and please to call me Patience, for I would like it so much more than 'my dear'!

"Um…yes, my…um…I mean Patience, but you see…I…" her husband tried to speak, but for some strange reason seemed unable to form a sentence.

"Oh Archie, please," she urged him and once more lifted her face to be kissed.

"Oh Patience!" he admitted hoarsely. "My darling Patience, I have wanted to kiss you for so long!"

Taking her in his arms and bowing his head, his lips touched hers, but then the door burst open again.

"Archie! You are right! It is great fun and…" cried Jasper but stopped talking at once. With an astonished look on his face, he turned and ran out of the room again.

So excited was Jasper, that he began to dance an impromptu jig in the hallway and Rip, finding that the master and mistress seemed to be far too busy to pay him any attention, ran around at his feet, barking happily with his tail wagging ecstatically.

"Cissy! Cissy!" Jasper yelled excitedly, "Come and look! Archie is kissing Patience!"

Printed in the United Kingdom
by Lightning Source UK Ltd.
121008UK00003B/250-294